GUINEA PIG

PET SHOP PRIVATE EYE

#4

Fish you Were Here

COLLEEN AF VENABLE

ILLUSTRATED BY
STEPHANIE YUE

GRAPHIC UNIVERSE™ · MINNEAPOLIS · NEW YORK

Story by Colleen AF Venable

Art by Stephanie Yue

Coloring by Hi-Fi Design

Lettering by Grace Lu

Graphic Universe™
A division of Lerner Publishing Group, Inc.
241 First Avenue North
Minneapolis, MN 55401 U.S.A.

Website address: www.lernerbooks.com

Main body text set in CCComicrazy.
Typeface provided by Comicraft/Active Images.

Library of Congress Cataloging-in-Publication Data

Venable, Colleen AF.
Fish you were here / by Colleen AF Venable ; illustrated by Stephanie Yue.
p. cm. — (Guinea PIG, pet shop private eye ; #4)
Summary: Guinea pig Sasspants knows something is wrong with ninth grader Viola, the new pet shop assistant, so when Mr. Venezi goes missing Sasspants and Hamisher put their private investigation skills to the test.
ISBN: 978–0–7613–5224–2 (lib. bdg. : alk. paper)
1. Graphic novels. [1. Graphic novels. 2. Mystery and detective stories. 3. Guinea pigs—Fiction. 4. Hamsters—Fiction. 5. Pet shops—Fiction. 6. Animals—Fiction. 7. Humorous stories.] I. Yue, Stephanie, ill. II. Title.
PZ7.7.V46Fis 2011
741.5'973—dc22 2011001079

Manufactured in the United States of America
1 – DP – 7/15/11

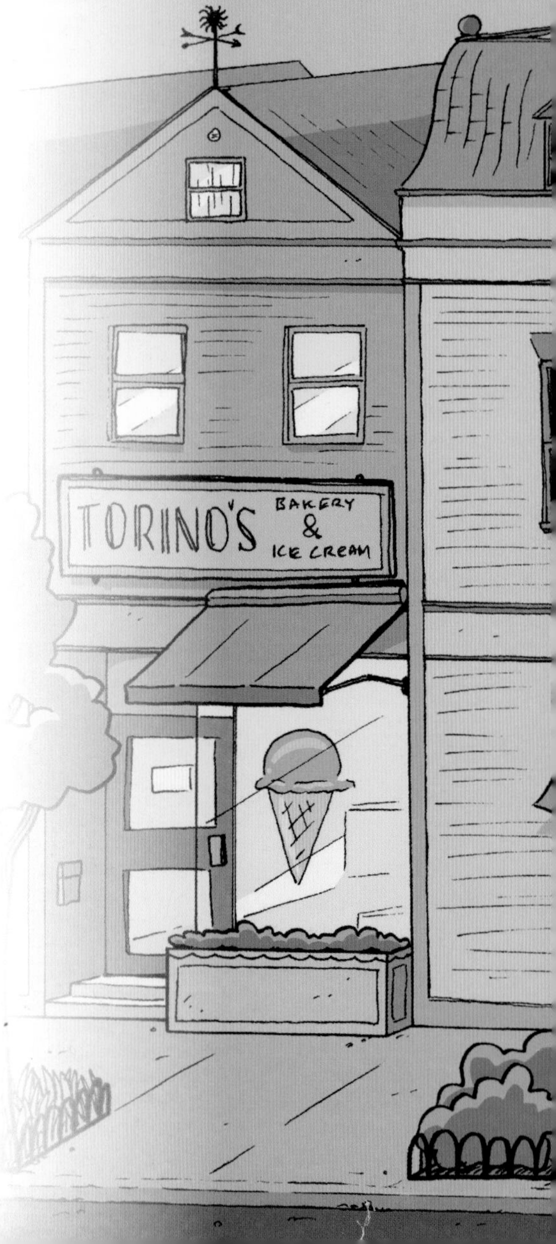
TORINO'S
BAKERY & ICE CREAM

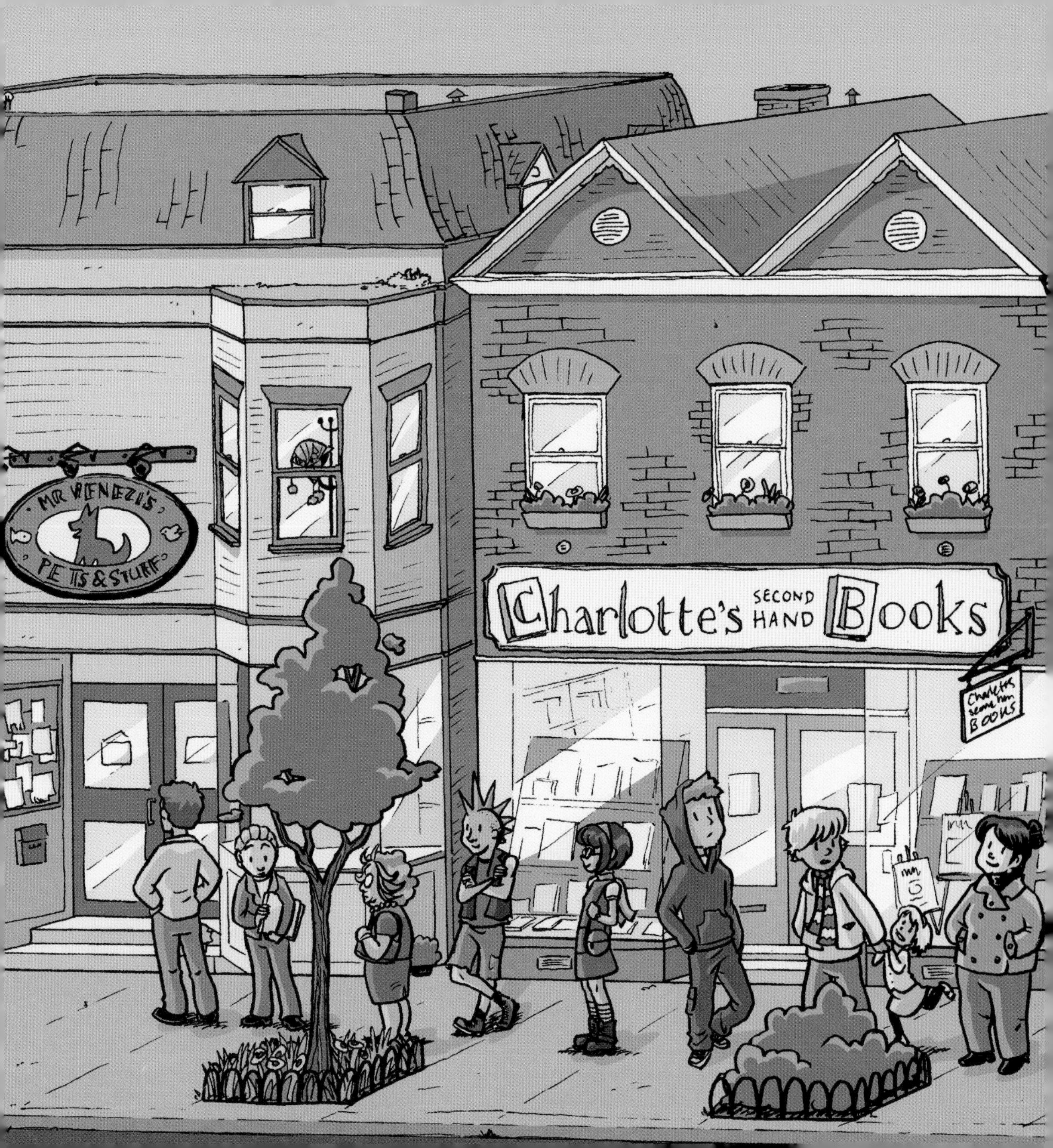
MR VENEZI'S
PETS & STUFF
Charlotte's SECOND HAND Books
Charlotte's second hand BOOKS

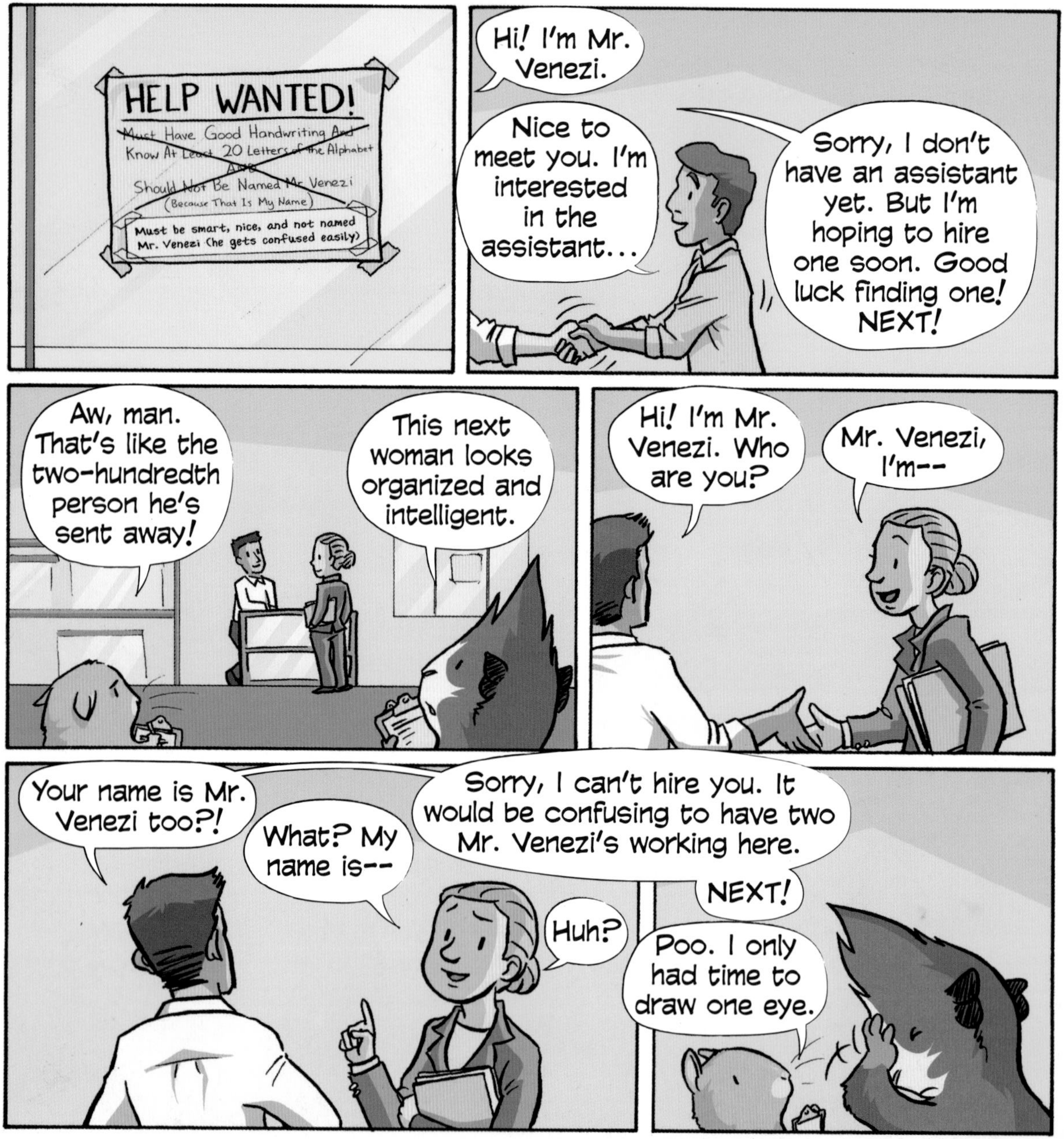
HELP WANTED!
Must Have Good Handwriting And Know At Least 20 Letters of the Alphabet And Should Not Be Named Mr Venezi (Because That Is My Name)
Must be smart, nice, and not named Mr. Venezi (he gets confused easily)
Hi! I'm Mr. Venezi.
Nice to meet you. I'm interested in the assistant...
Sorry, I don't have an assistant yet. But I'm hoping to hire one soon. Good luck finding one! NEXT!
Aw, man. That's like the two-hundredth person he's sent away!
This next woman looks organized and intelligent.
Hi! I'm Mr. Venezi. Who are you?
Mr. Venezi, I'm--
Your name is Mr. Venezi too?!
What? My name is--
Sorry, I can't hire you. It would be confusing to have two Mr. Venezi's working here.
NEXT!
Huh?
Poo. I only had time to draw one eye.

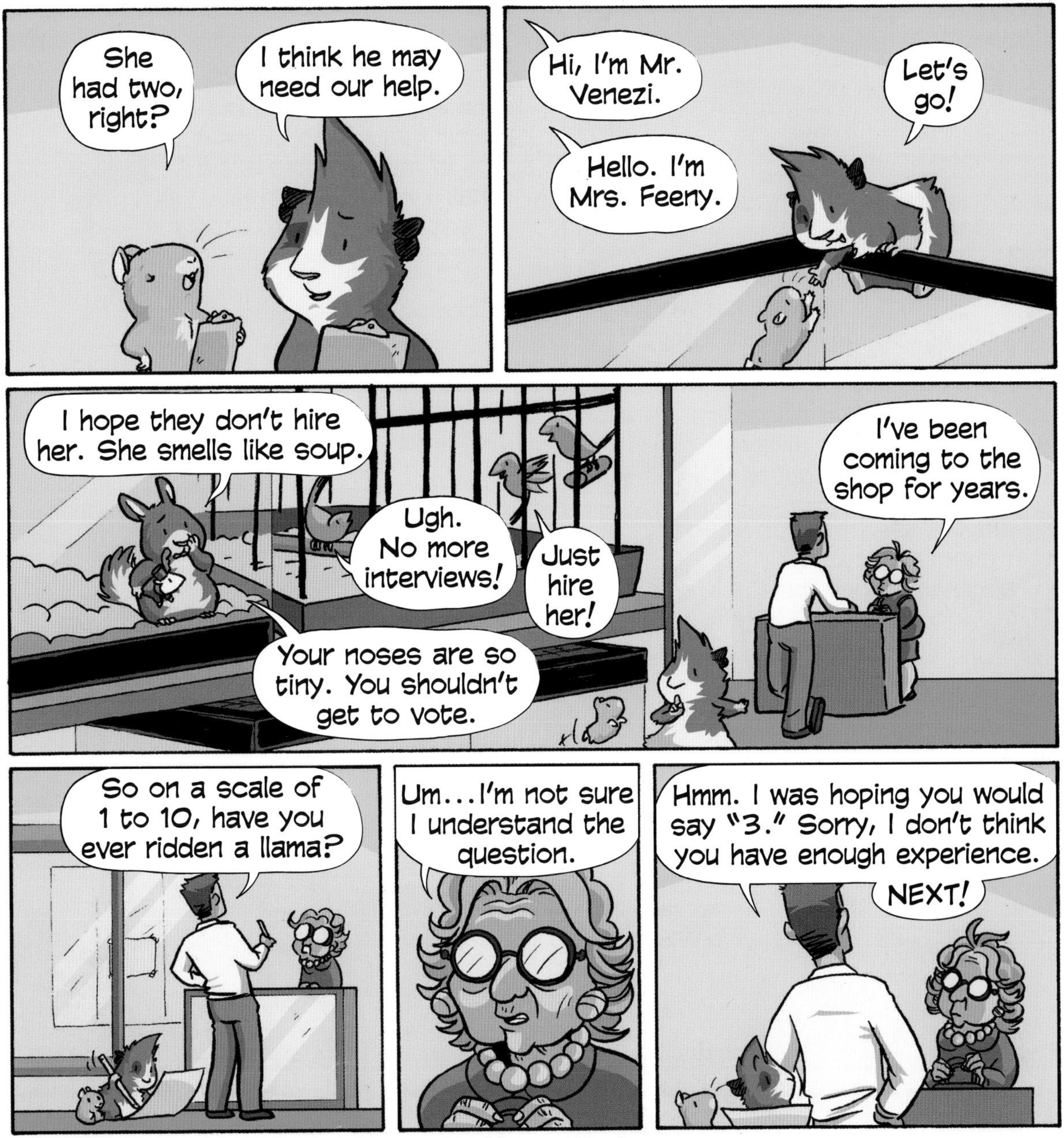
She had two, right?
I think he may need our help.
Hi, I'm Mr. Venezi.
Hello. I'm Mrs. Feeny.
Let's go!
I hope they don't hire her. She smells like soup.
Ugh. No more interviews!
Just hire her!
Your noses are so tiny. You shouldn't get to vote.
I've been coming to the shop for years.
So on a scale of 1 to 10, have you ever ridden a llama?
Um...I'm not sure I understand the question.
Hmm. I was hoping you would say "3." Sorry, I don't think you have enough experience.
NEXT!

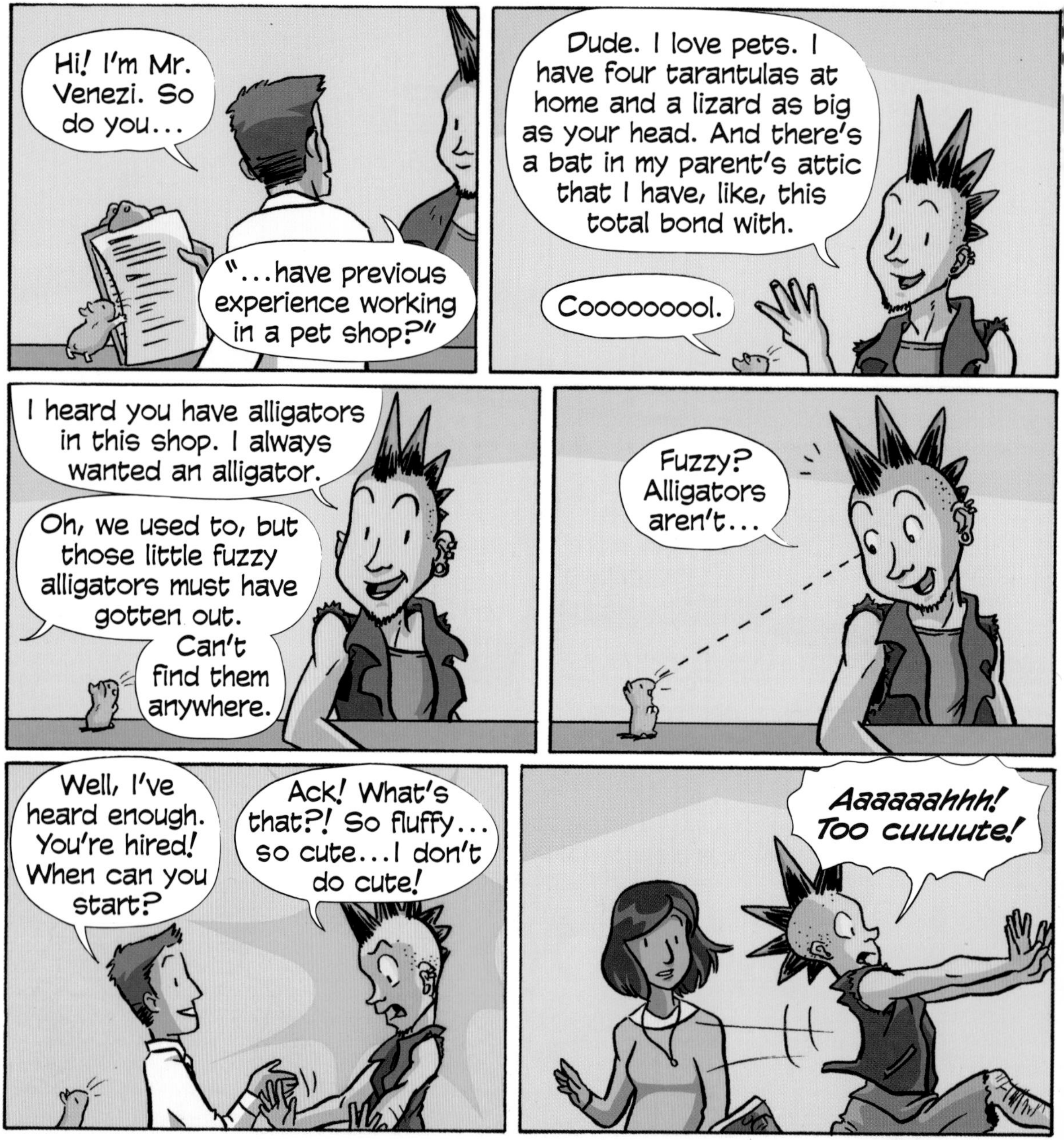
Hi! I'm Mr. Venezi. So do you...
"...have previous experience working in a pet shop?"
Dude. I love pets. I have four tarantulas at home and a lizard as big as your head. And there's a bat in my parent's attic that I have, like, this total bond with.
Cooooooool.
I heard you have alligators in this shop. I always wanted an alligator.
Oh, we used to, but those little fuzzy alligators must have gotten out.
Can't find them anywhere.
Fuzzy? Alligators aren't...
Well, I've heard enough. You're hired! When can you start?
Ack! What's that?! So fluffy... so cute...I don't do cute!
Aaaaaahhh! Too cuuuute!

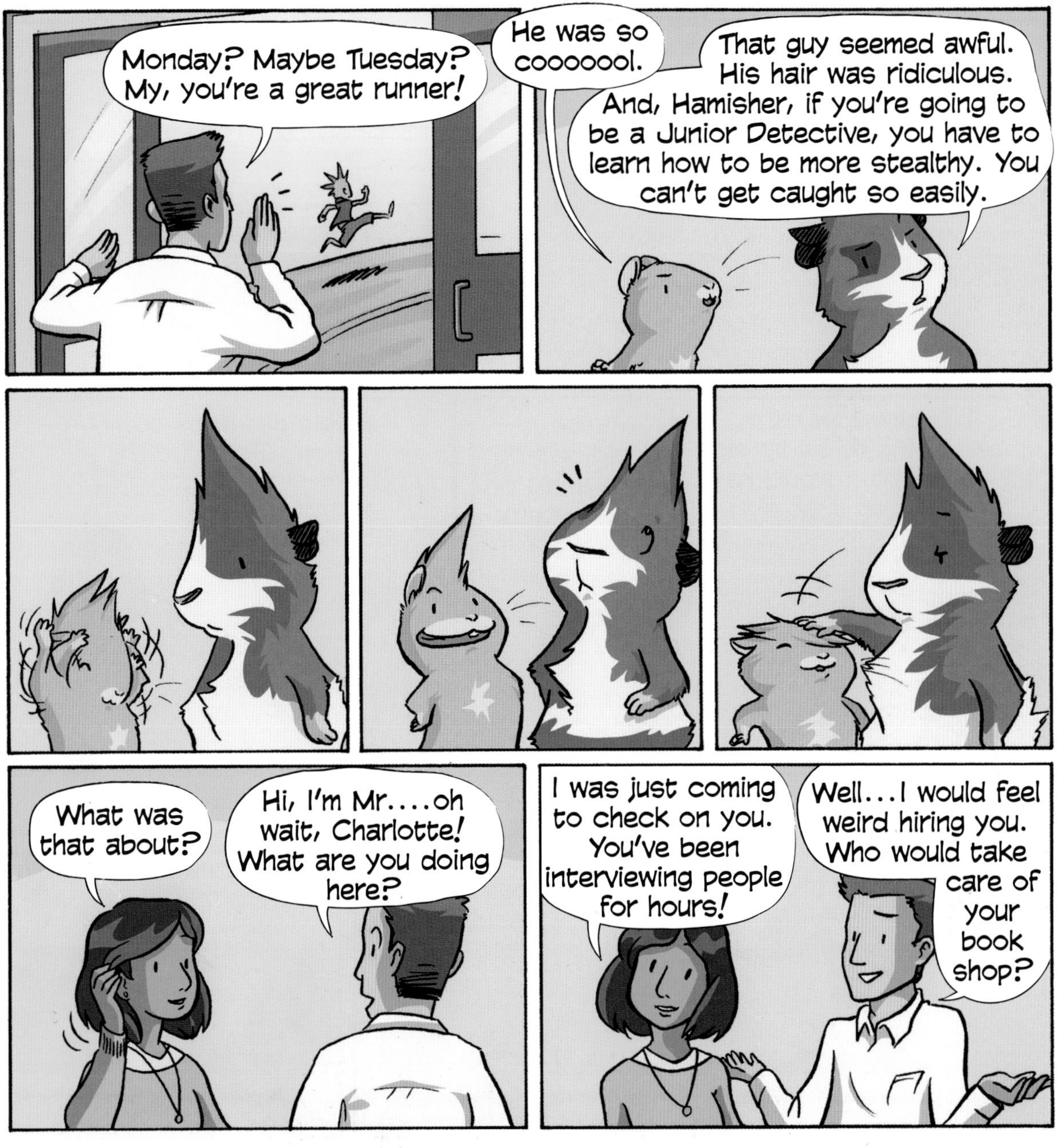
Monday? Maybe Tuesday? My, you're a great runner!
He was so coooooool.
That guy seemed awful. His hair was ridiculous. And, Hamisher, if you're going to be a Junior Detective, you have to learn how to be more stealthy. You can't get caught so easily.
What was that about?
Hi, I'm Mr.... oh wait, Charlotte! What are you doing here?
I was just coming to check on you. You've been interviewing people for hours!
Well... I would feel weird hiring you. Who would take care of your book shop?

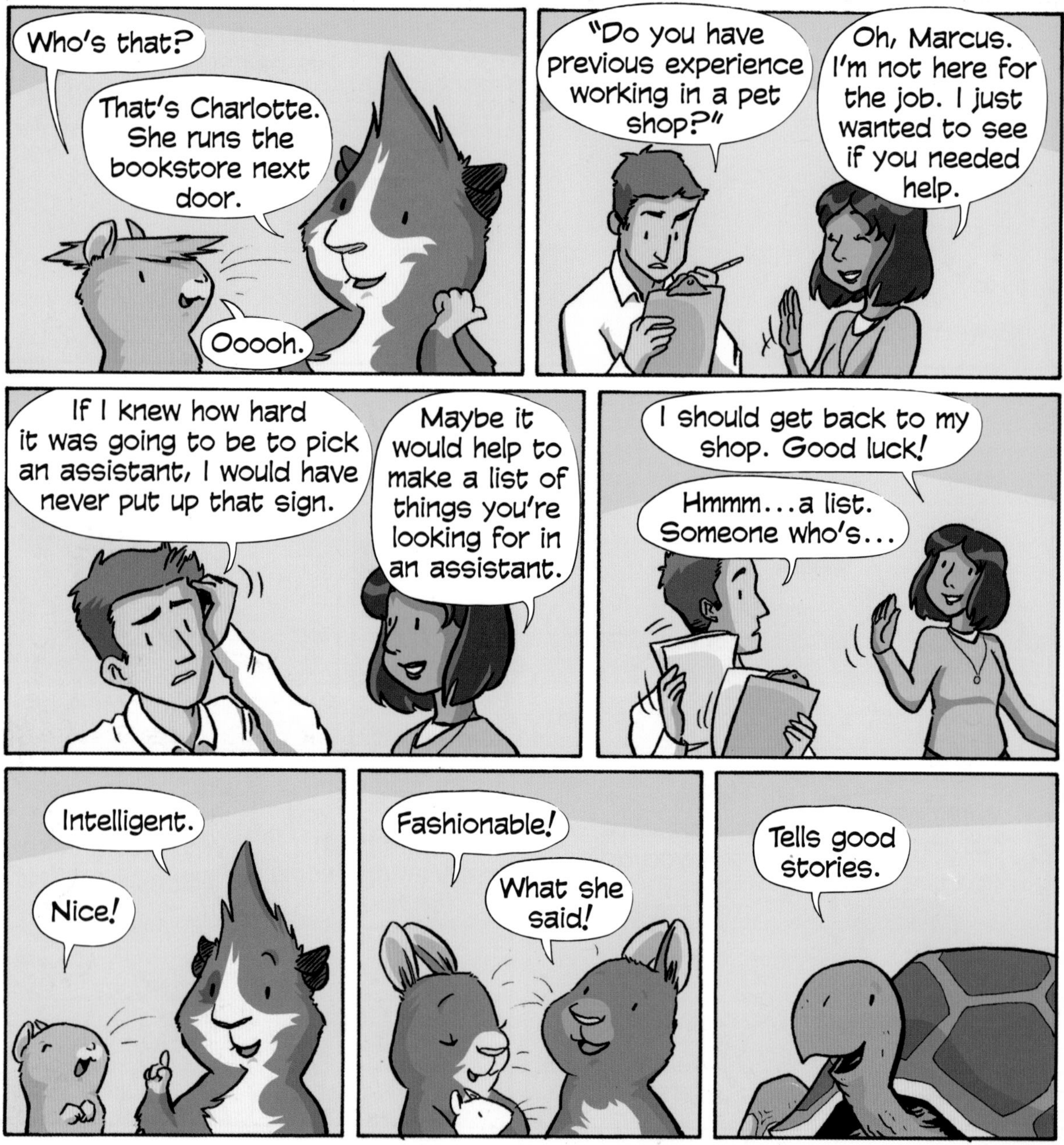
Who's that?
That's Charlotte. She runs the bookstore next door.
Ooooh.
"Do you have previous experience working in a pet shop?"
Oh, Marcus. I'm not here for the job. I just wanted to see if you needed help.
If I knew how hard it was going to be to pick an assistant, I would have never put up that sign.
Maybe it would help to make a list of things you're looking for in an assistant.
I should get back to my shop. Good luck!
Hmmm...a list. Someone who's...
Intelligent.
Nice!
Fashionable!
What she said!
Tells good stories.

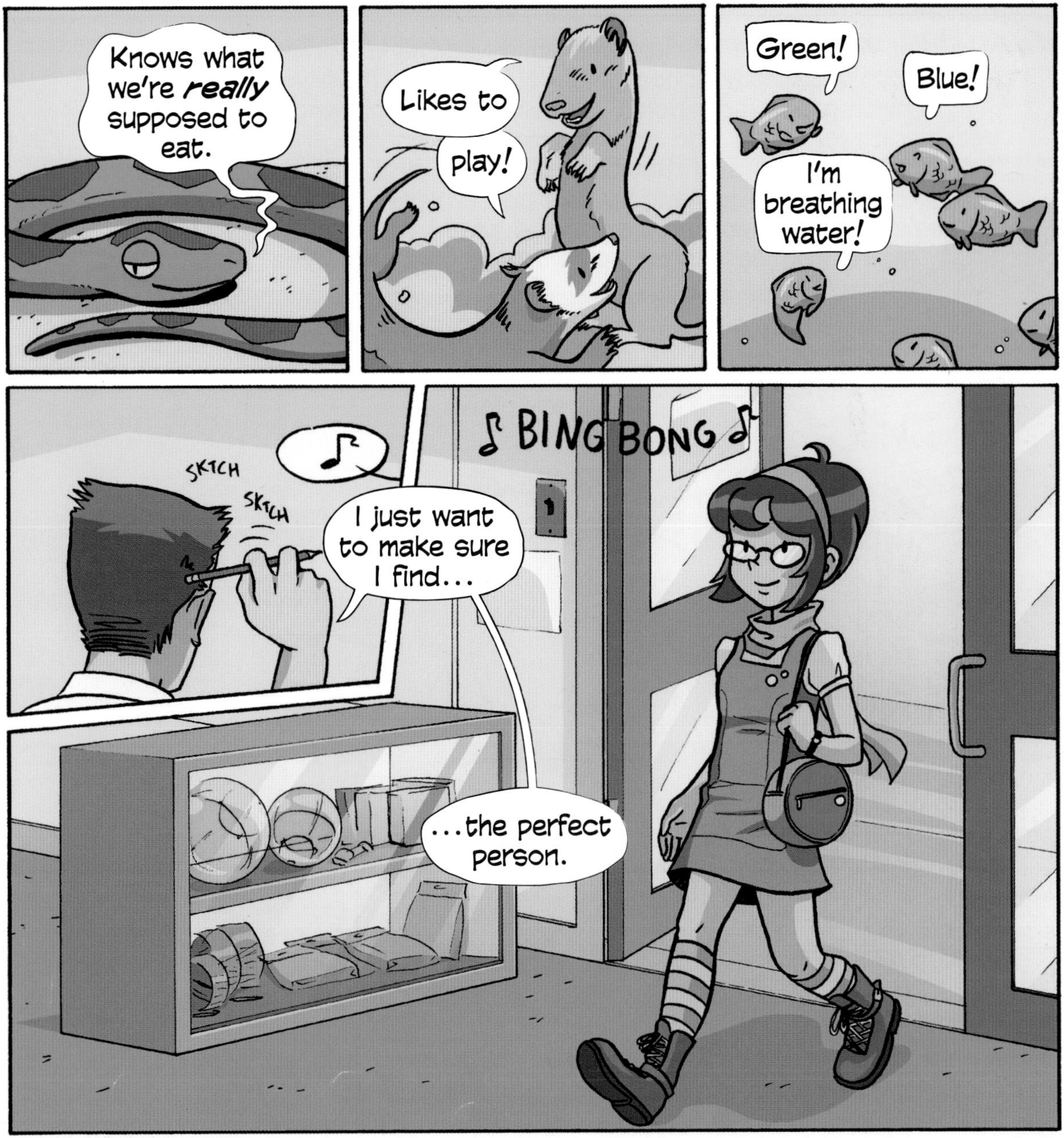
Knows what we're *really* supposed to eat.
Likes to
play!
Green!
Blue!
I'm breathing water!
SKTCH
SKTCH
I just want to make sure I find...
BING BONG
...the perfect person.

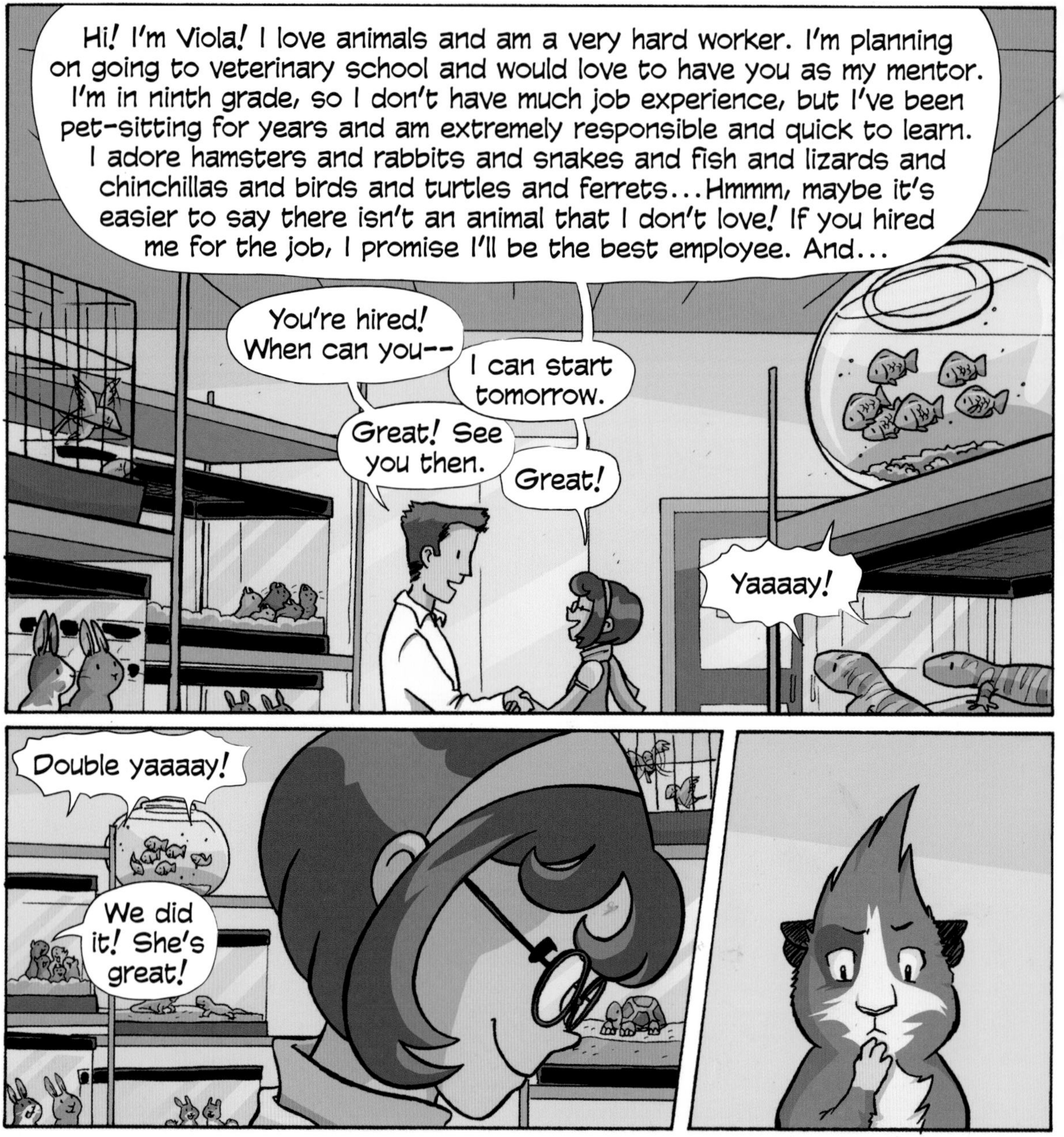
Hi! I'm Viola! I love animals and am a very hard worker. I'm planning on going to veterinary school and would love to have you as my mentor. I'm in ninth grade, so I don't have much job experience, but I've been pet-sitting for years and am extremely responsible and quick to learn. I adore hamsters and rabbits and snakes and fish and lizards and chinchillas and birds and turtles and ferrets... Hmmm, maybe it's easier to say there isn't an animal that I don't love! If you hired me for the job, I promise I'll be the best employee. And...
You're hired! When can you--
I can start tomorrow.
Great! See you then.
Great!
Yaaaay!
Double yaaaay!
We did it! She's great!

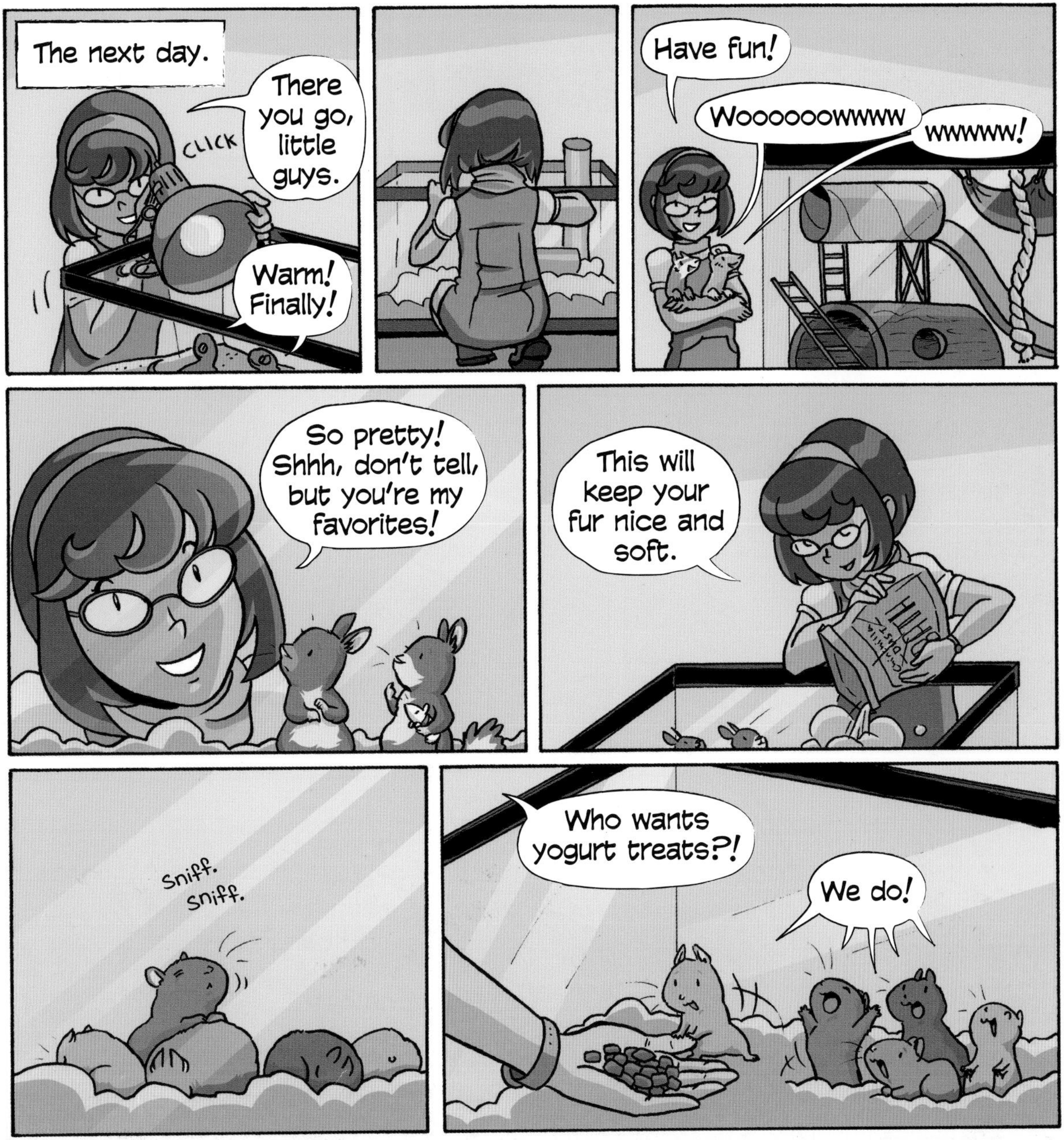
The next day.
There you go, little guys.
CLICK
Warm! Finally!
Have fun!
Woooooowwww
wwwww!
So pretty! Shhh, don't tell, but you're my favorites!
This will keep your fur nice and soft.
Sniff.
Sniff.
Who wants yogurt treats?!
We do!

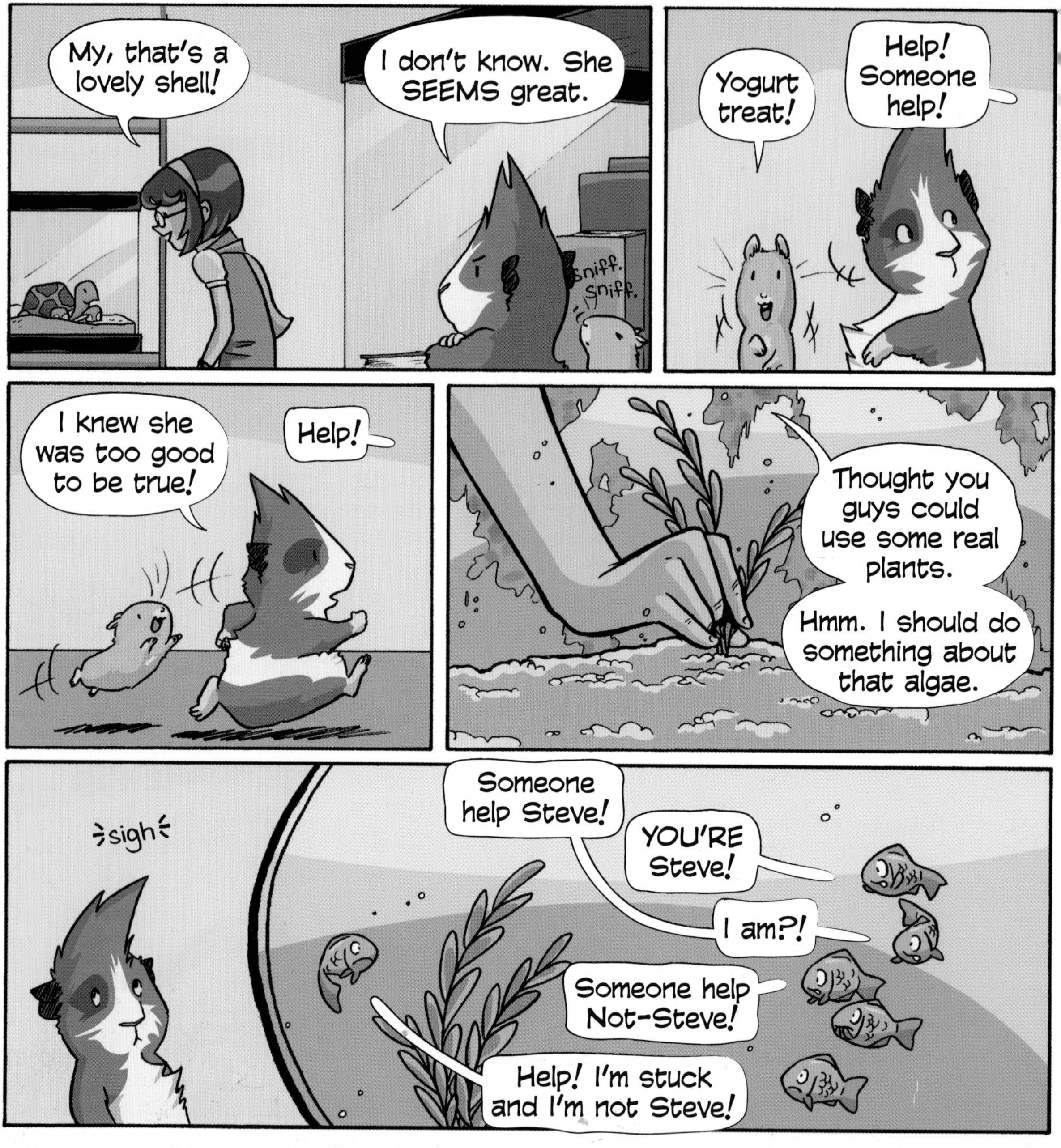
My, that's a lovely shell!
I don't know. She SEEMS great.
Sniff. Sniff.
Yogurt treat!
Help! Someone help!
I knew she was too good to be true!
Help!
Thought you guys could use some real plants.
Hmm. I should do something about that algae.
sigh
Someone help Steve!
YOU'RE Steve!
I am?!
Someone help Not-Steve!
Help! I'm stuck and I'm not Steve!

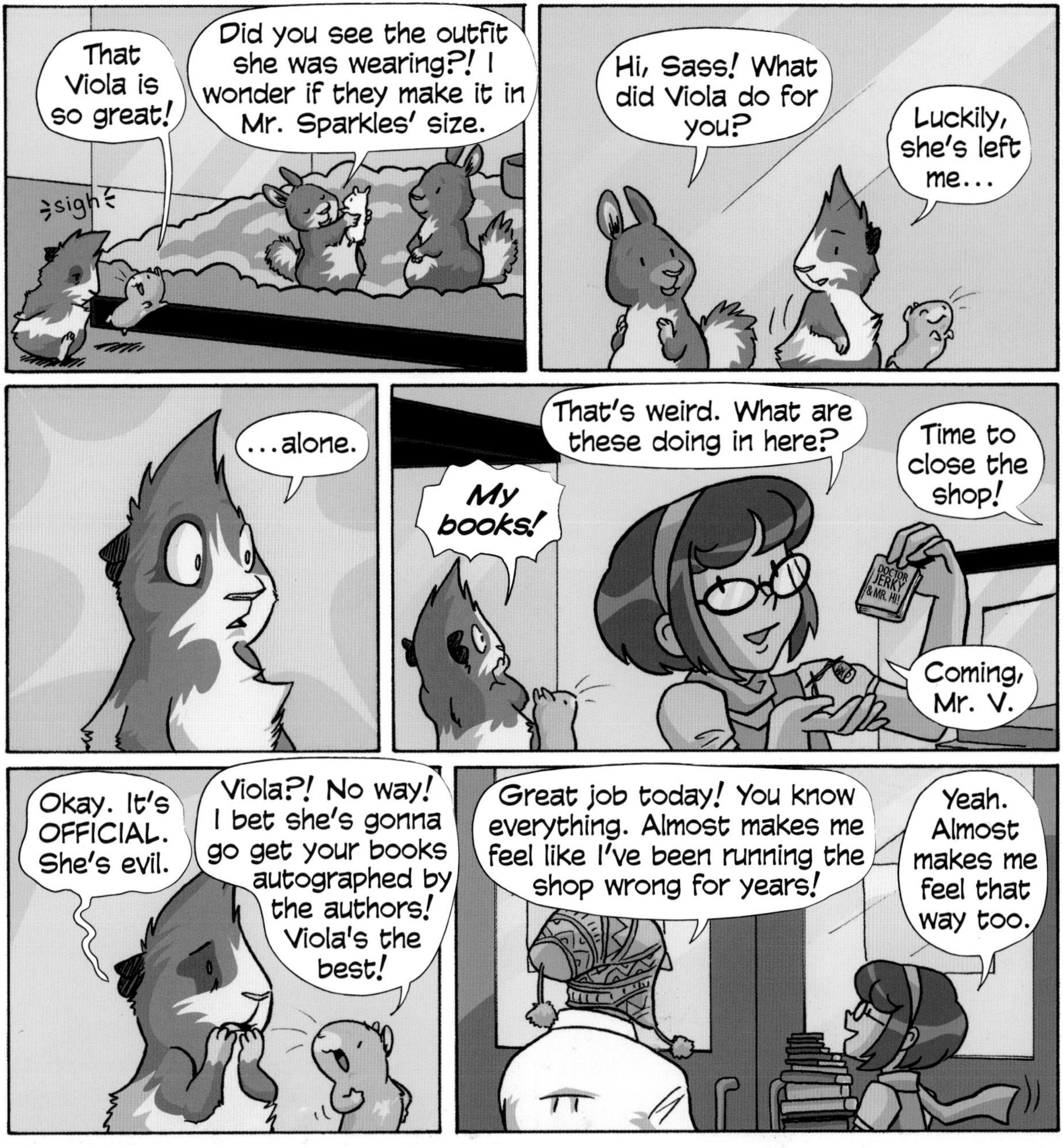
That Viola is so great!
Did you see the outfit she was wearing?! I wonder if they make it in Mr. Sparkles' size.
sigh
Hi, Sass! What did Viola do for you?
Luckily, she's left me...
...alone.
That's weird. What are these doing in here?
Time to close the shop!
My books!
DOCTOR JERKY & MR. HI!
Coming, Mr. V.
Okay. It's OFFICIAL. She's evil.
Viola?! No way! I bet she's gonna go get your books autographed by the authors! Viola's the best!
Great job today! You know everything. Almost makes me feel like I've been running the shop wrong for years!
Yeah. Almost makes me feel that way too.

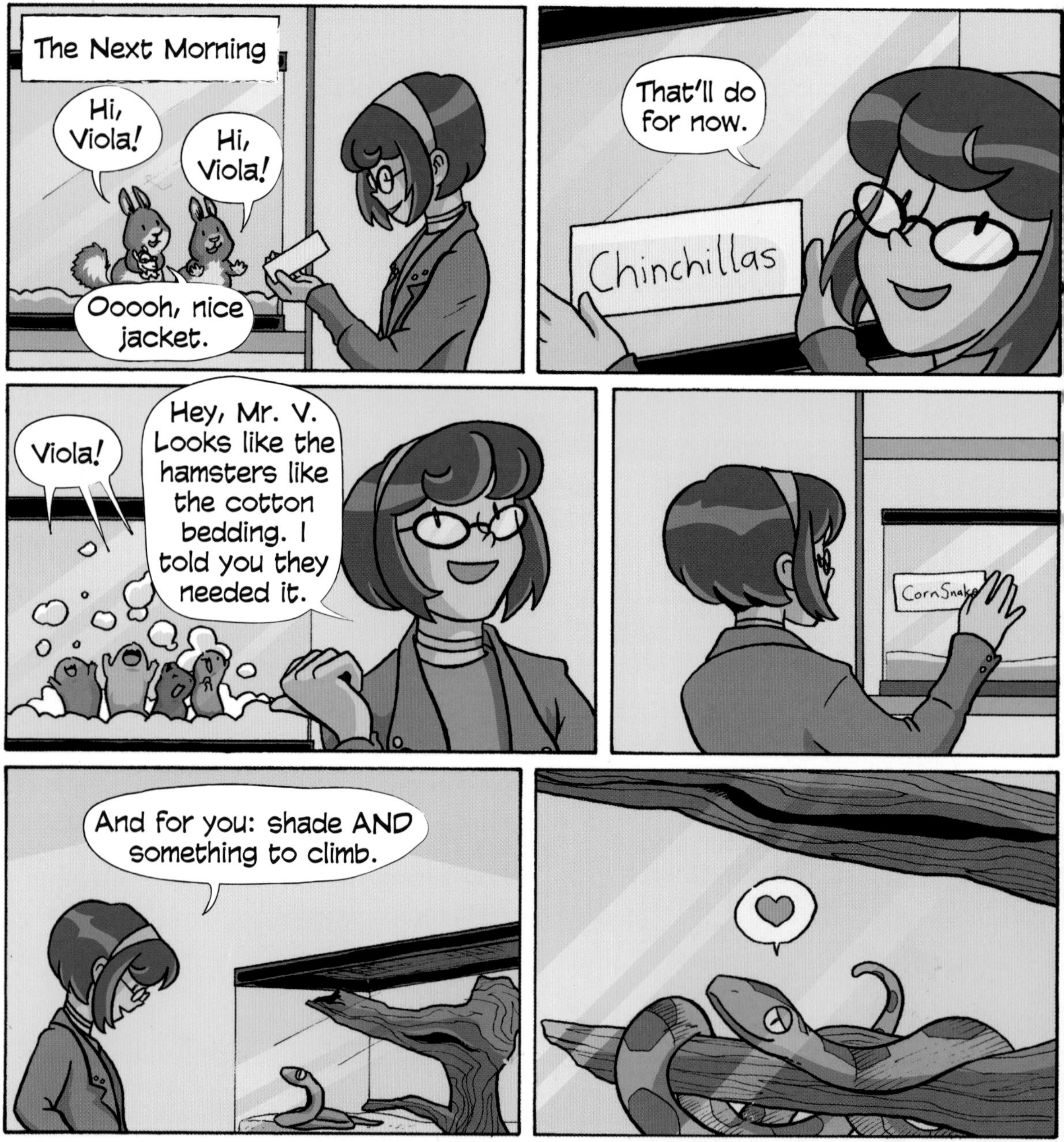
The Next Morning
Hi, Viola!
Hi, Viola!
Ooooh, nice jacket.
That'll do for now.
Chinchillas
Viola!
Hey, Mr. V. Looks like the hamsters like the cotton bedding. I told you they needed it.
CornSnake
And for you: shade AND something to climb.

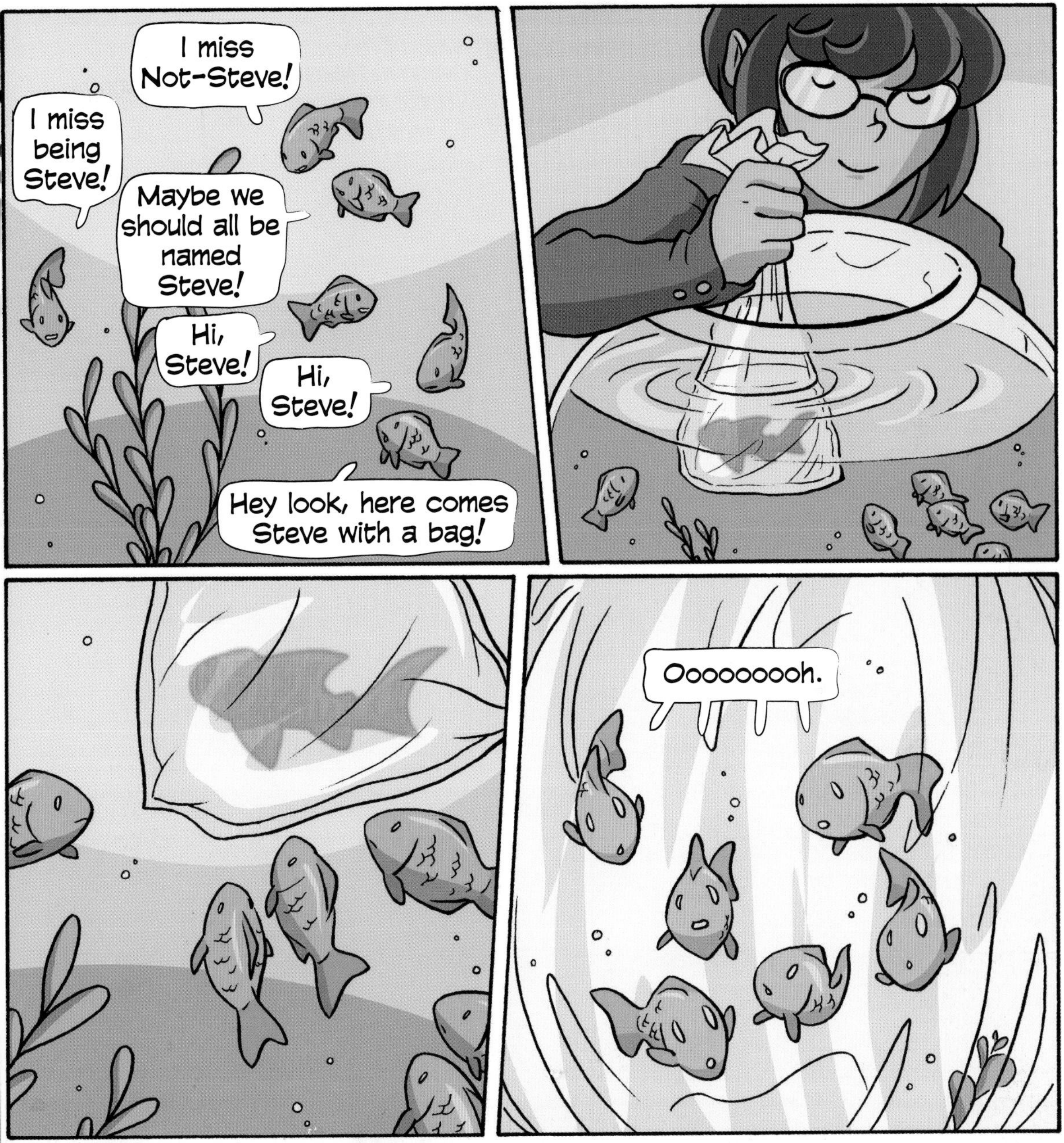
I miss Not-Steve!
I miss being Steve!
Maybe we should all be named Steve!
Hi, Steve!
Hi, Steve!
Hey look, here comes Steve with a bag!
Ooooooooh.

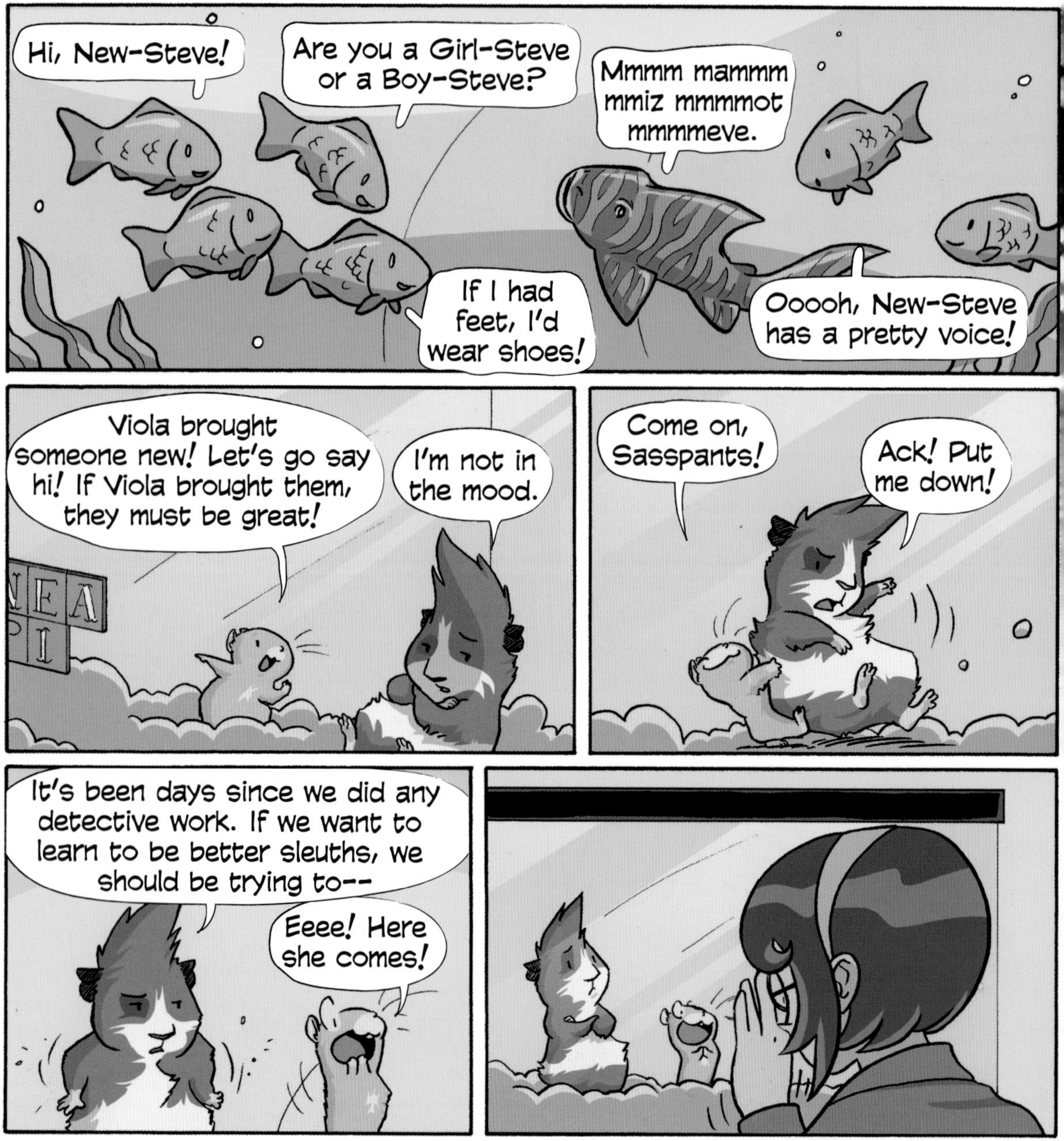
Hi, New-Steve!
Are you a Girl-Steve or a Boy-Steve?
Mmmm mammm mmiz mmmmot mmmmeve.
If I had feet, I'd wear shoes!
Ooooh, New-Steve has a pretty voice!
Viola brought someone new! Let's go say hi! If Viola brought them, they must be great!
I'm not in the mood.
NEA
PI
Come on, Sasspants!
Ack! Put me down!
It's been days since we did any detective work. If we want to learn to be better sleuths, we should be trying to--
Eeee! Here she comes!

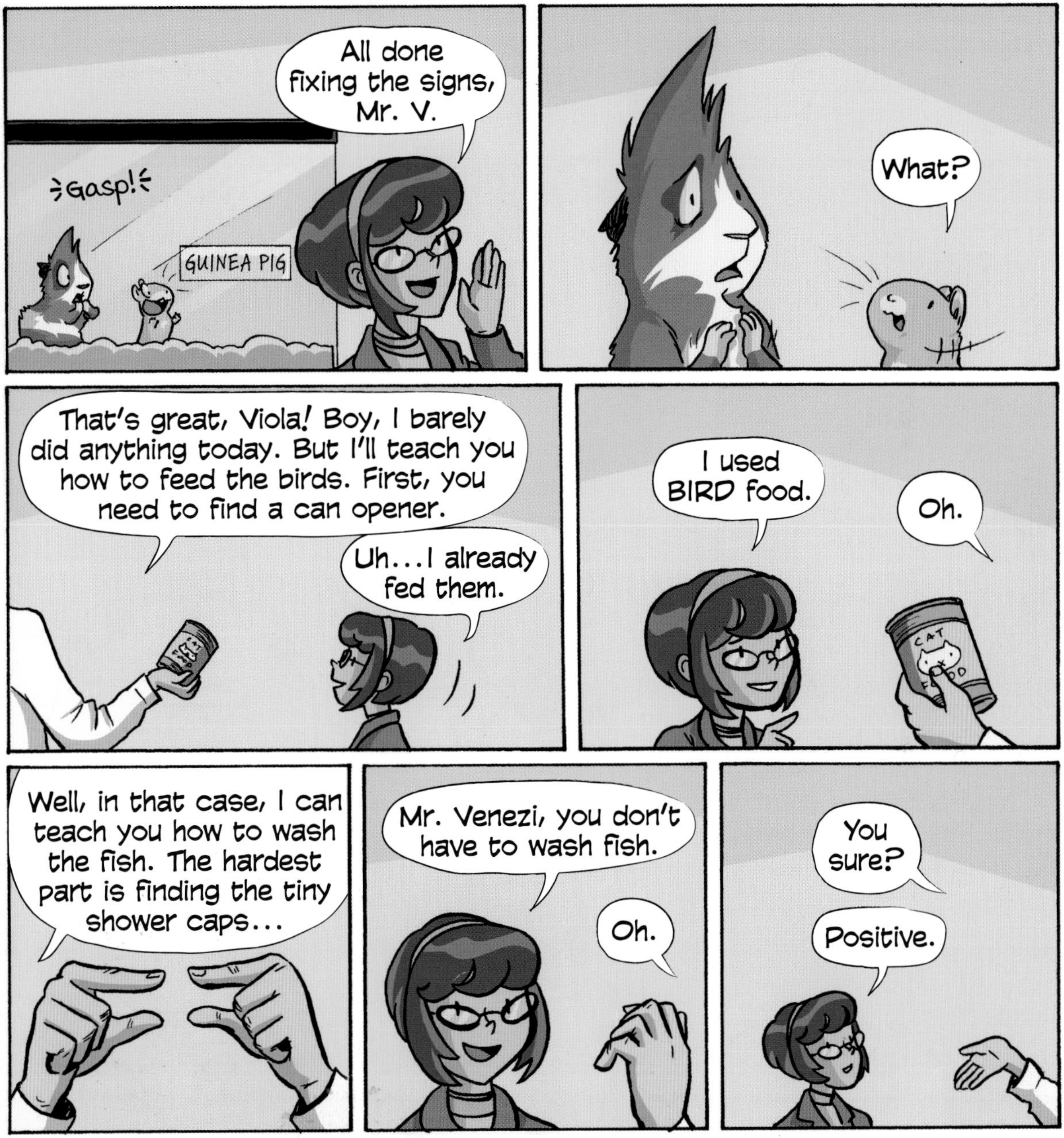
All done fixing the signs, Mr. V.
Gasp!
GUINEA PIG
What?
That's great, Viola! Boy, I barely did anything today. But I'll teach you how to feed the birds. First, you need to find a can opener.
Uh...I already fed them.
CAT FOOD
I used BIRD food.
Oh.
CAT FOOD
Well, in that case, I can teach you how to wash the fish. The hardest part is finding the tiny shower caps...
Mr. Venezi, you don't have to wash fish.
Oh.
You sure?
Positive.

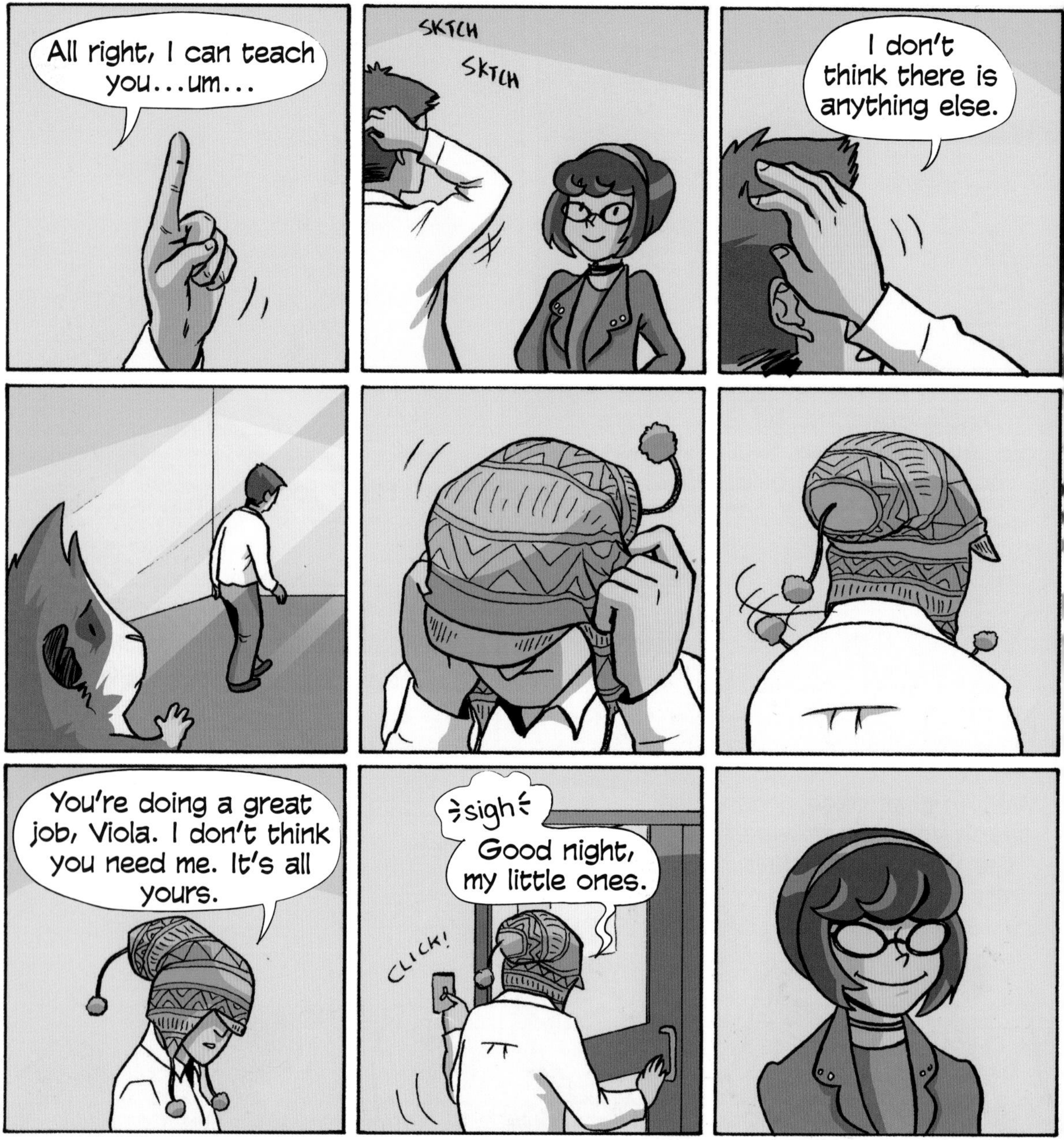
All right, I can teach you...um...
SKTCH
SKTCH
I don't think there is anything else.
You're doing a great job, Viola. I don't think you need me. It's all yours.
sigh
Good night, my little ones.
CLICK!

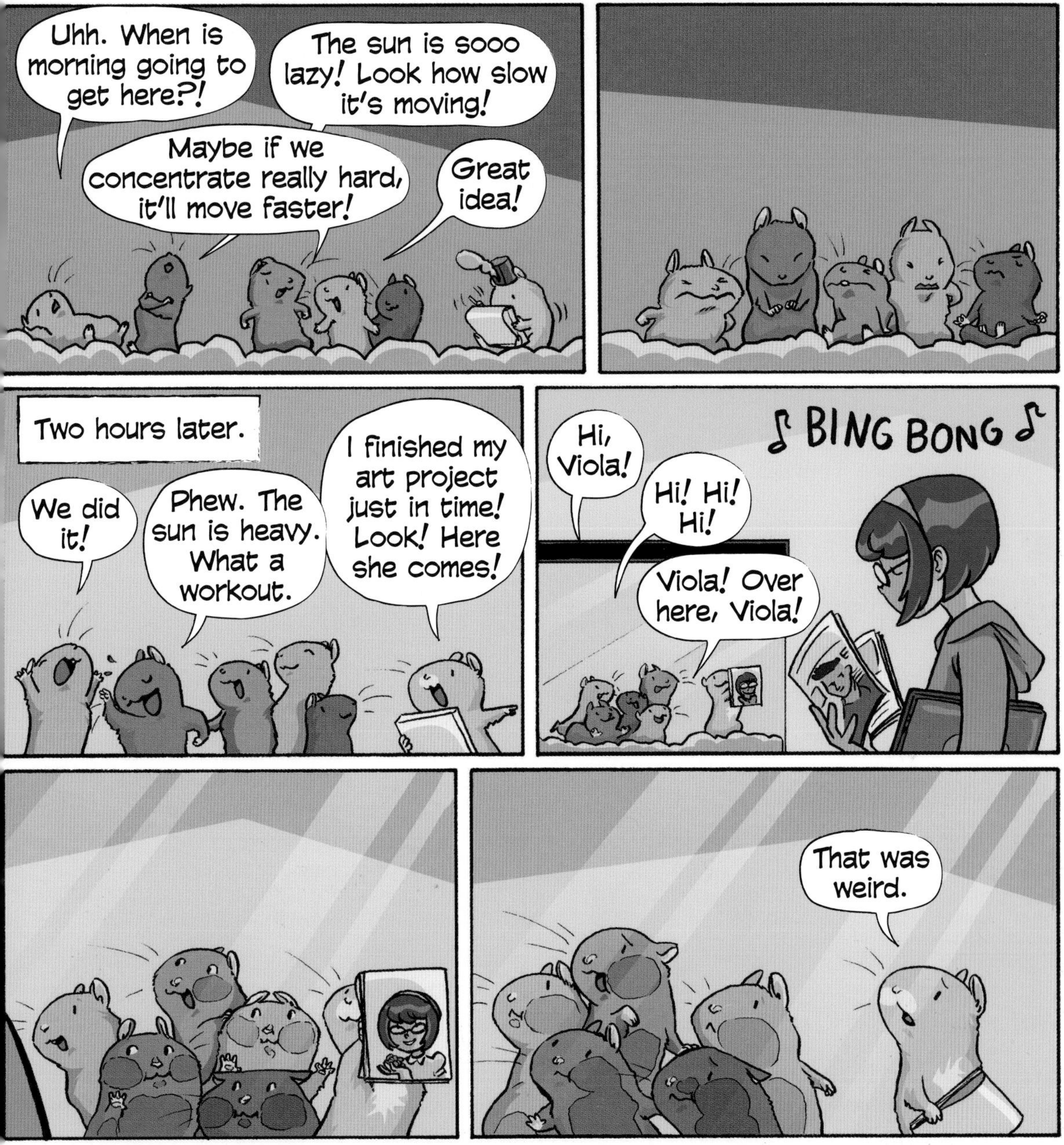
Uhh. When is morning going to get here?!
The sun is sooo lazy! Look how slow it's moving!
Maybe if we concentrate really hard, it'll move faster!
Great idea!
Two hours later.
We did it!
Phew. The sun is heavy. What a workout.
I finished my art project just in time! Look! Here she comes!
BING BONG
Hi, Viola!
Hi! Hi! Hi!
Viola! Over here, Viola!
That was weird.

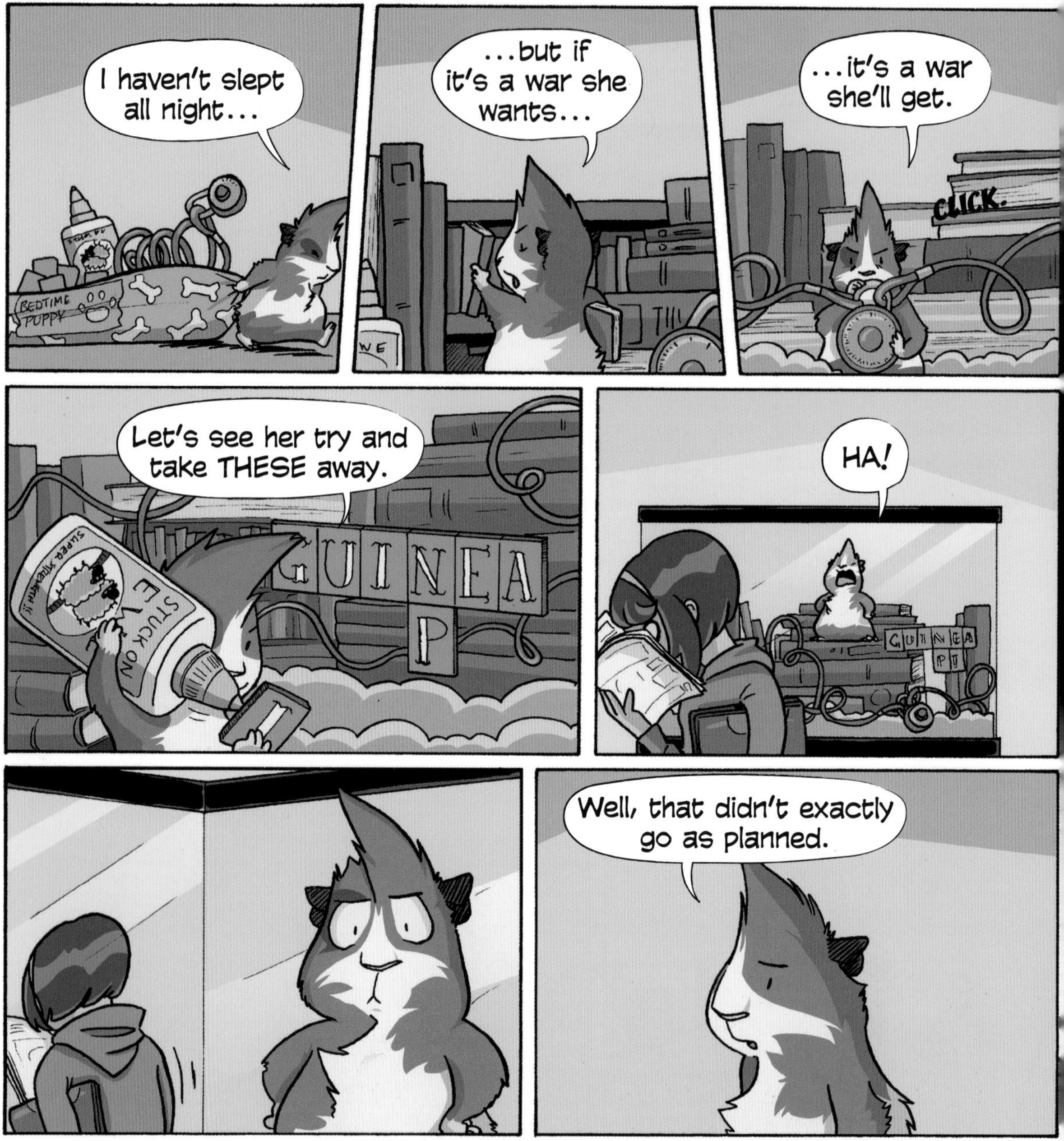
I haven't slept all night...
BEDTIME PUPPY
...but if it's a war she wants...
...it's a war she'll get.
CLICK.
Let's see her try and take THESE away.
STUCK ON
GUINEA
P
HA!
Well, that didn't exactly go as planned.

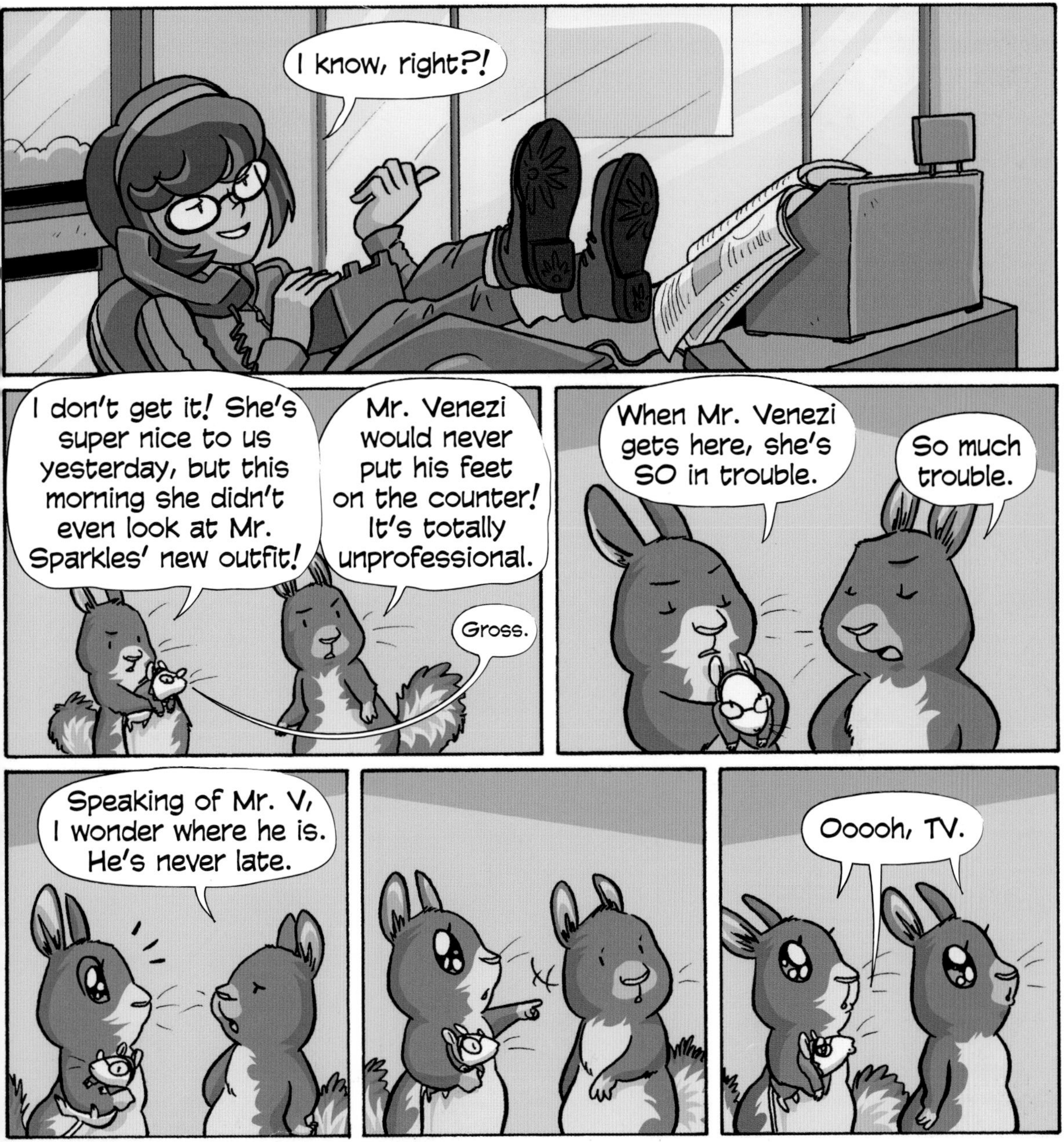
I know, right?!
I don't get it! She's super nice to us yesterday, but this morning she didn't even look at Mr. Sparkles' new outfit!
Mr. Venezi would never put his feet on the counter! It's totally unprofessional.
Gross.
When Mr. Venezi gets here, she's SO in trouble.
So much trouble.
Speaking of Mr. V, I wonder where he is. He's never late.
Ooooh, TV.

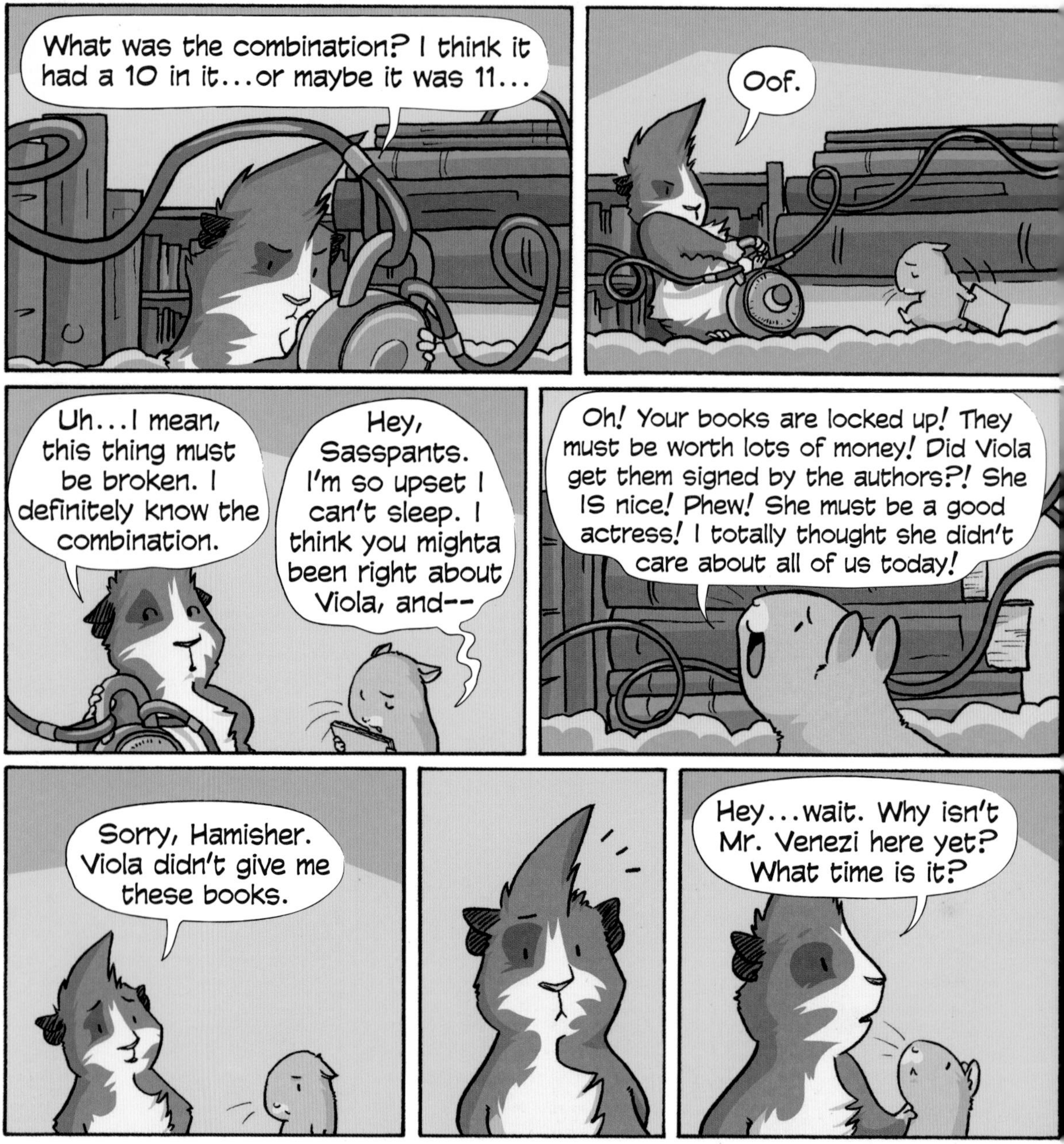
What was the combination? I think it had a 10 in it...or maybe it was 11...
Oof.
Uh...I mean, this thing must be broken. I definitely know the combination.
Hey, Sasspants. I'm so upset I can't sleep. I think you mighta been right about Viola, and--
Oh! Your books are locked up! They must be worth lots of money! Did Viola get them signed by the authors?! She IS nice! Phew! She must be a good actress! I totally thought she didn't care about all of us today!
Sorry, Hamisher. Viola didn't give me these books.
Hey...wait. Why isn't Mr. Venezi here yet? What time is it?

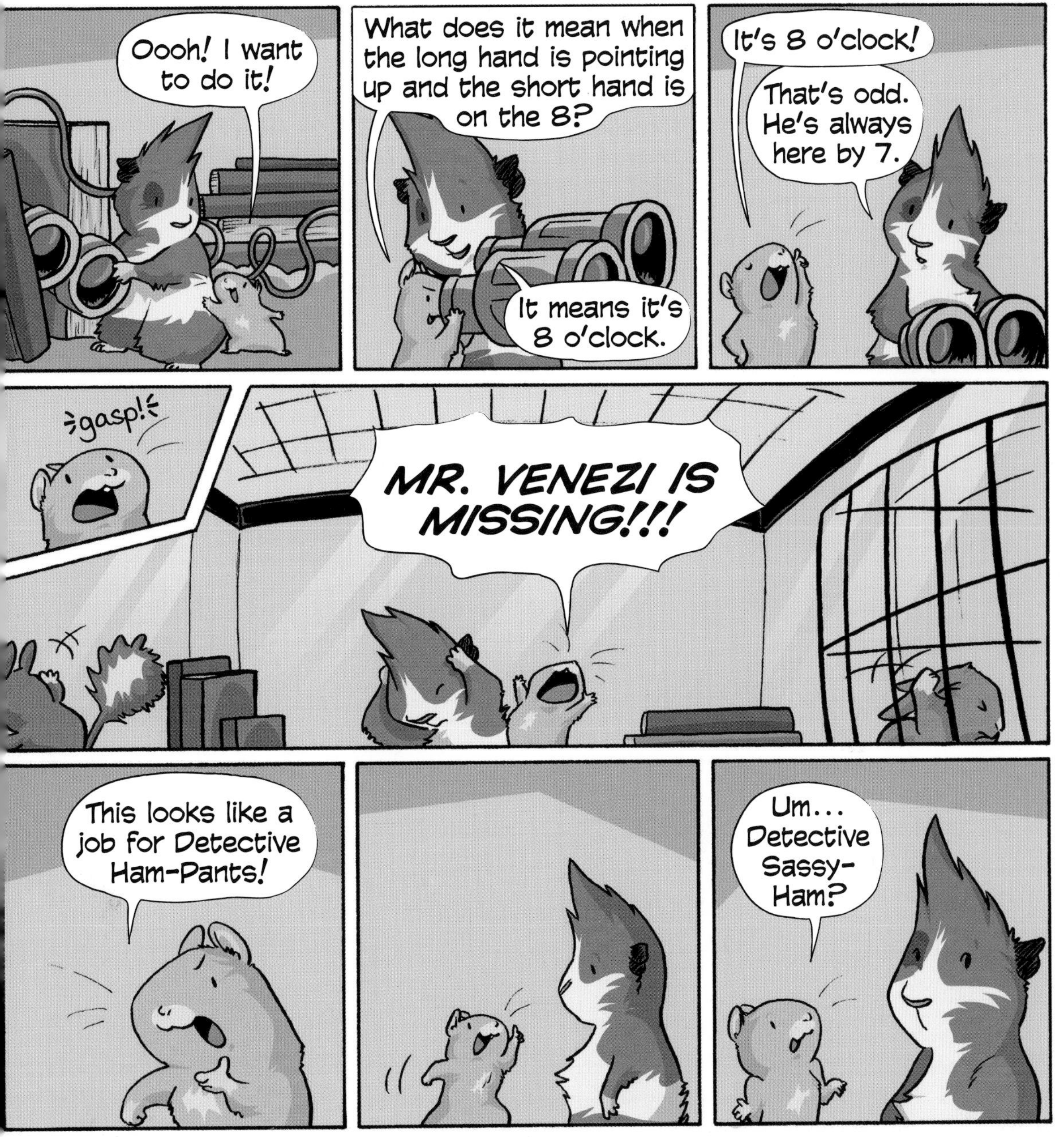

Oooh! I want to do it!
What does it mean when the long hand is pointing up and the short hand is on the 8?
It means it's 8 o'clock.
It's 8 o'clock!
That's odd. He's always here by 7.
gasp!
MR. VENEZI IS MISSING!!!
This looks like a job for Detective Ham-Pants!
Um... Detective Sassy-Ham?

Or if you don't like those, we can always just use our real names.

Though, if we use our real names, I'd like to change mine to Dragon.

I'm sure Mr. V's sleeping late or something. Maybe he forgot to set his alarm.

We should do interviews and find out if anyone's seen him!

To the fish!

Why do we always start with the fish? You know they never know anything...or at least they can't remember it.

They make me feel smart.

Well, you ARE a Junior Detective now. So if you want to interview the fish first, then that's what we'll do.

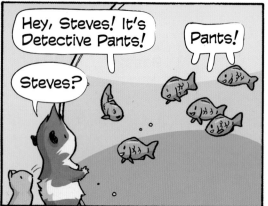

Hey, Steves! It's Detective Pants!

Steves?

Pants!

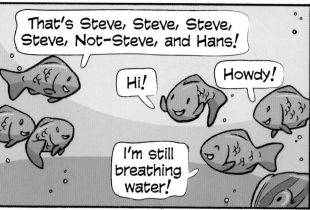

That's Steve, Steve, Steve, Steve, Not-Steve, and Hans!

Hi!

Howdy!

I'm still breathing water!

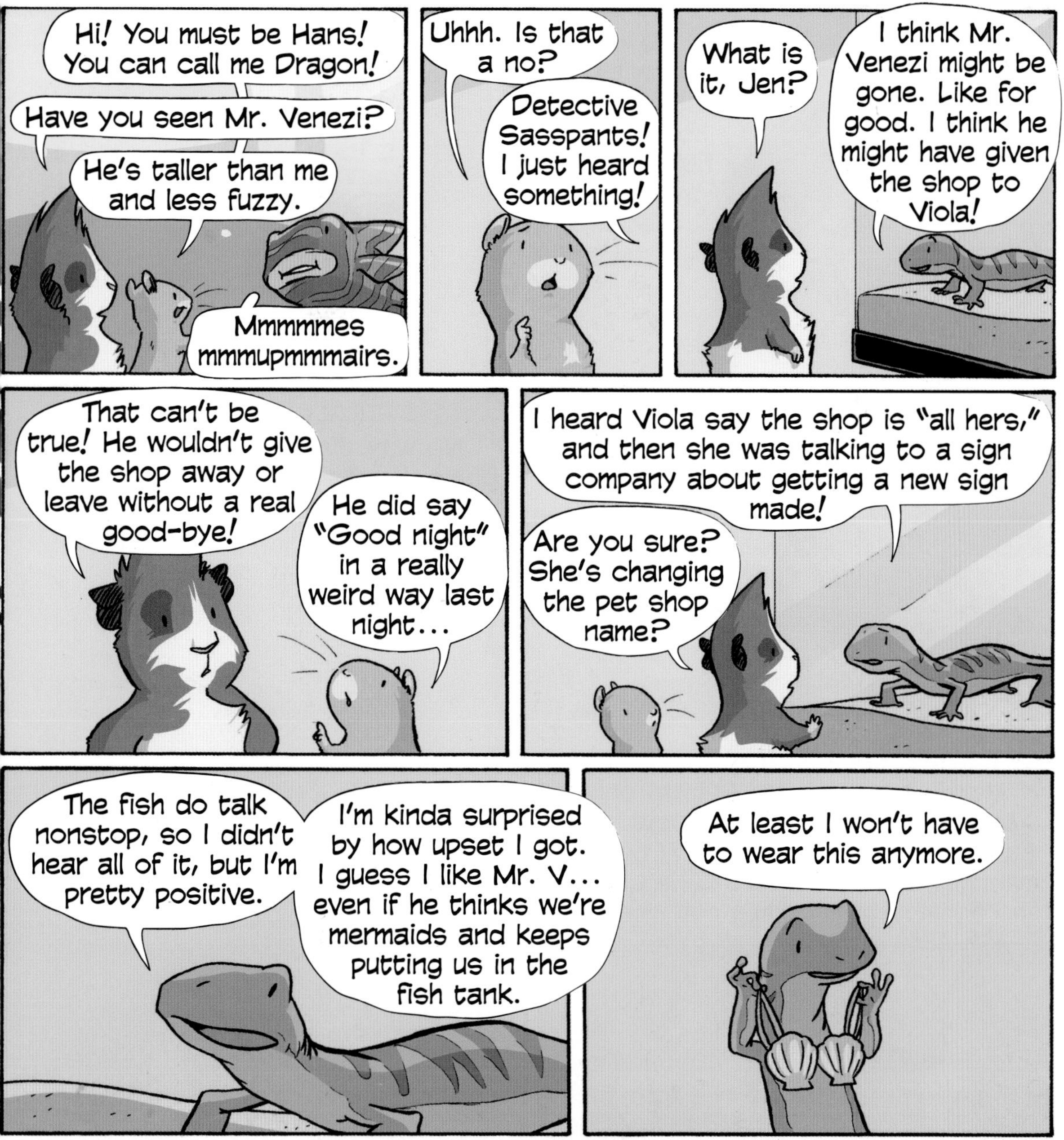
Hi! You must be Hans! You can call me Dragon!
Have you seen Mr. Venezi?
He's taller than me and less fuzzy.
Mmmmmes mmmupmmmairs.
Uhhh. Is that a no?
Detective Sasspants! I just heard something!
What is it, Jen?
I think Mr. Venezi might be gone. Like for good. I think he might have given the shop to Viola!
That can't be true! He wouldn't give the shop away or leave without a real good-bye!
He did say "Good night" in a really weird way last night...
I heard Viola say the shop is "all hers," and then she was talking to a sign company about getting a new sign made!
Are you sure? She's changing the pet shop name?
The fish do talk nonstop, so I didn't hear all of it, but I'm pretty positive.
I'm kinda surprised by how upset I got. I guess I like Mr. V... even if he thinks we're mermaids and keeps putting us in the fish tank.
At least I won't have to wear this anymore.

I can't believe Mr. V gave us all away!

We don't know that's true. You know how much the fish talk. I bet those lizards misheard.

I wish there was someone closer to the desk.

Um... I think there is.

No way. I'm not going to work hard if I don't have to!

What's going on?

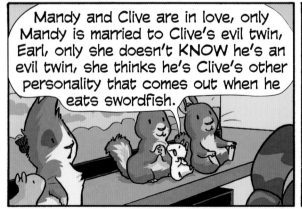

Mandy and Clive are in love, only Mandy is married to Clive's evil twin, Earl, only she doesn't KNOW he's an evil twin, she thinks he's Clive's other personality that comes out when he eats swordfish.

Mr. Venezi is missing! And we detectives can't stop until we detectivize where he is!

I really like this show.

Missing? Are you sure? It's only 10 am. Maybe he had a dentist appointment.

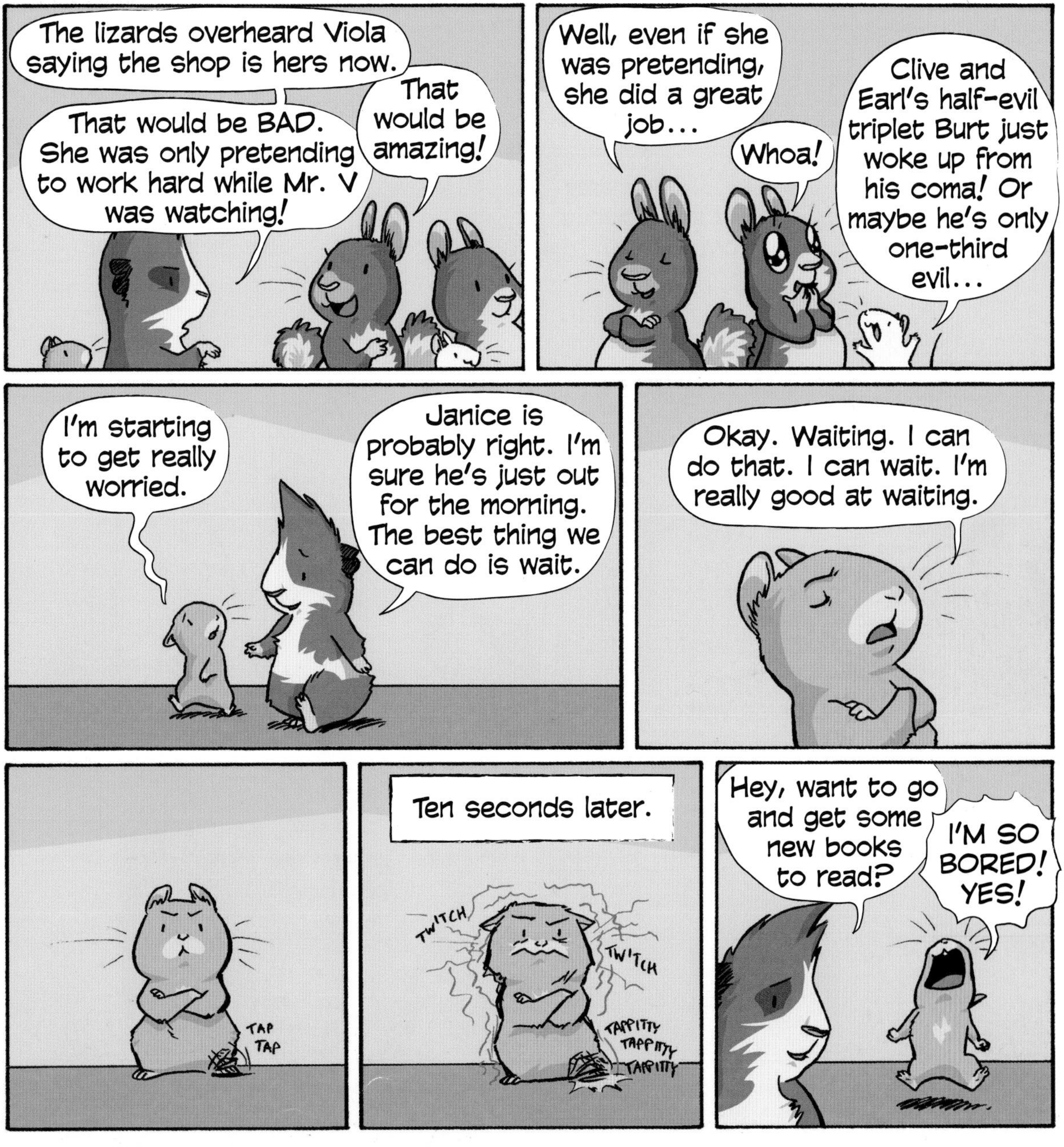

The lizards overheard Viola saying the shop is hers now.
That would be BAD. She was only pretending to work hard while Mr. V was watching!
That would be amazing!
Well, even if she was pretending, she did a great job...
Whoa!
Clive and Earl's half-evil triplet Burt just woke up from his coma! Or maybe he's only one-third evil...
I'm starting to get really worried.
Janice is probably right. I'm sure he's just out for the morning. The best thing we can do is wait.
Okay. Waiting. I can do that. I can wait. I'm really good at waiting.
TAP TAP
Ten seconds later.
TWITCH
TWITCH
TAPPITTY TAPPITTY TAPPITTY
Hey, want to go and get some new books to read?
I'M SO BORED! YES!

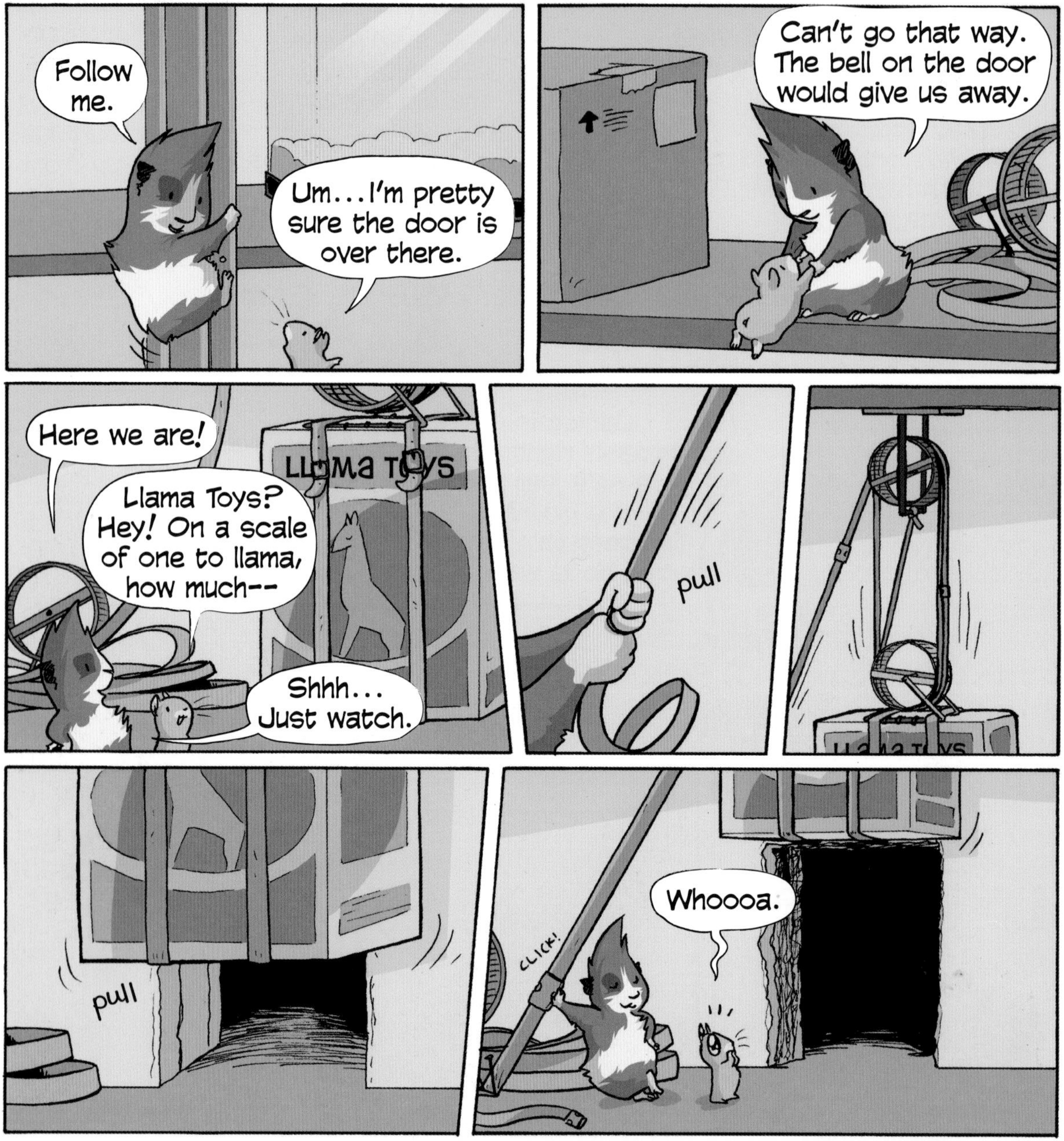
Follow me.
Um...I'm pretty sure the door is over there.
Can't go that way. The bell on the door would give us away.
Here we are!
LLAMA TOYS
Llama Toys? Hey! On a scale of one to llama, how much--
Shhh... Just watch.
pull
pull
CLICK!
Whoooa.

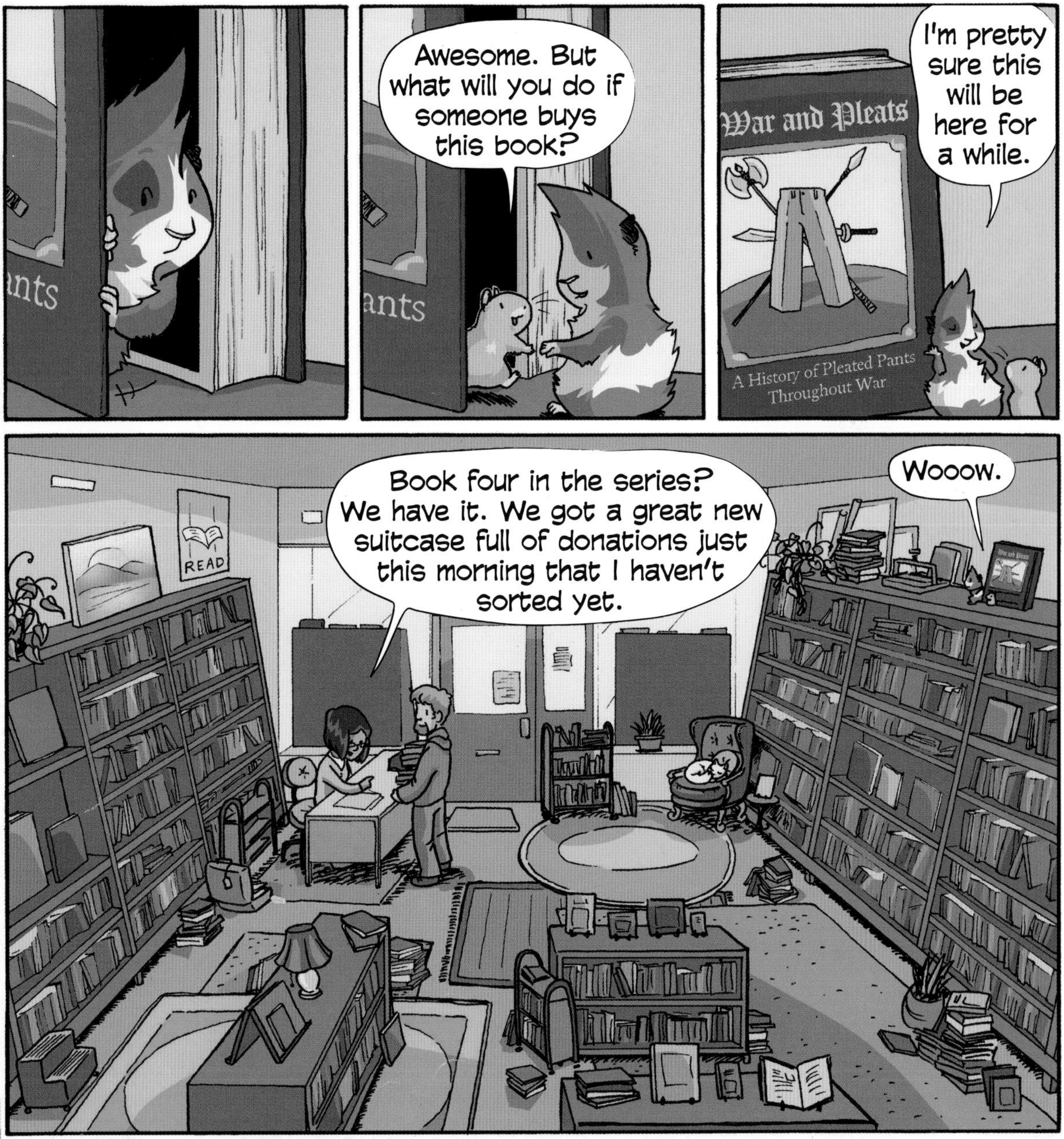
ants
ants
Awesome. But what will you do if someone buys this book?
War and Pleats
A History of Pleated Pants Throughout War
I'm pretty sure this will be here for a while.
READ
Book four in the series? We have it. We got a great new suitcase full of donations just this morning that I haven't sorted yet.
Wooow.

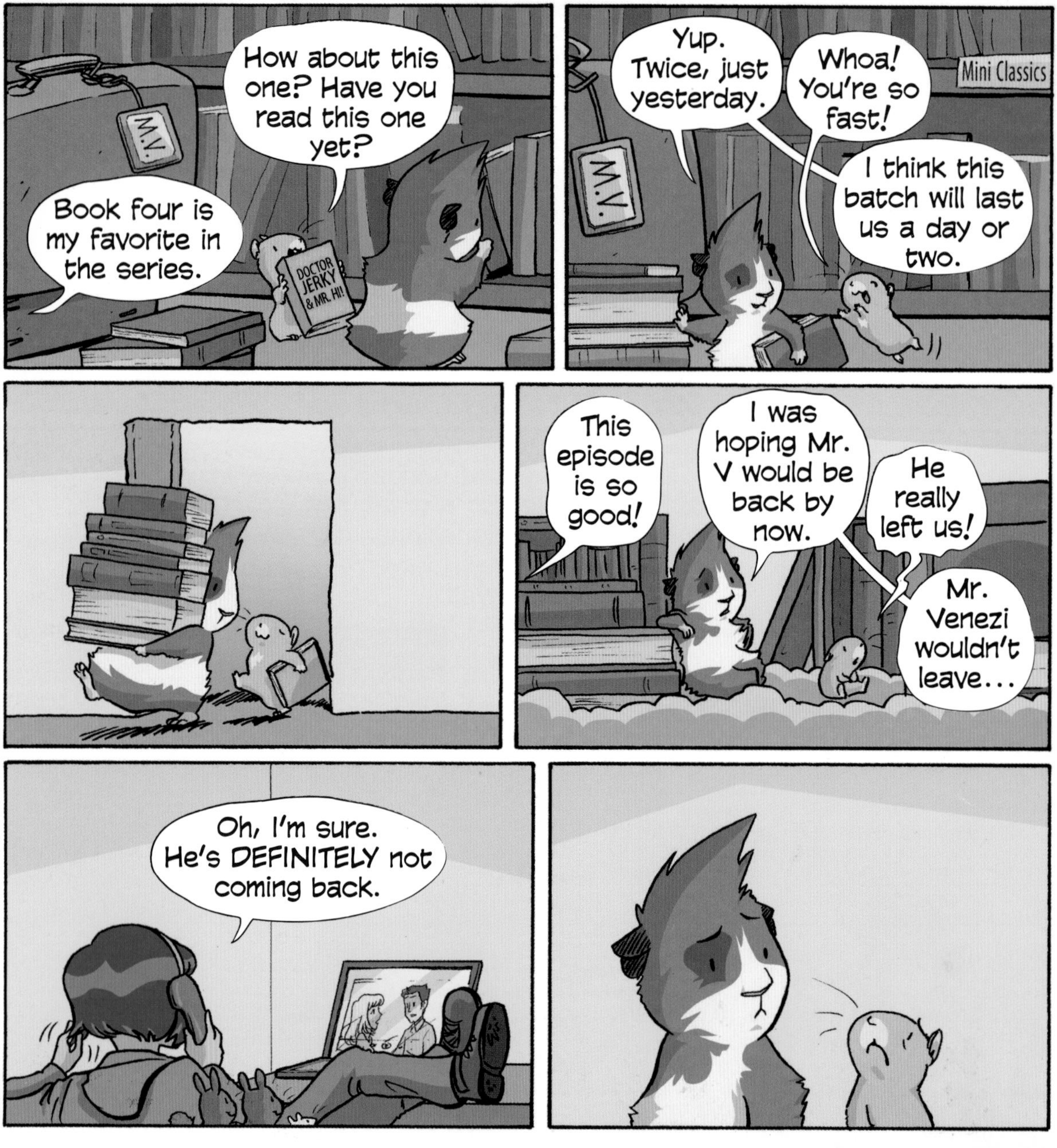
M.V.
How about this one? Have you read this one yet?
Book four is my favorite in the series.
DOCTOR JERKY & MR. HI!
Mini Classics
M.V.
Yup. Twice, just yesterday.
Whoa! You're so fast!
I think this batch will last us a day or two.
This episode is so good!
I was hoping Mr. V would be back by now.
He really left us!
Mr. Venezi wouldn't leave...
Oh, I'm sure. He's DEFINITELY not coming back.

This is no longer fun. It doesn't make sense.

He doesn't love us anymore! And Viola never really loved us! I wish we never made that papier-mâché sculpture of her head!

Huh?

Um...never mind.

We need to find Mr. Venezi and make him come back.

I, for one, am happy he's gone. Look at what she gave me.

Your water dish is almost empty.

So is your sidekick's lovely little head. The difference is, Viola can fix MY problem.

Lovely? Thanks! I use conditioner.

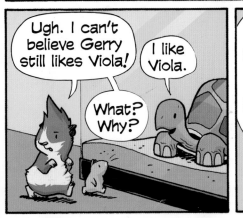

Ugh. I can't believe Gerry still likes Viola!

I like Viola.

What? Why?

She's been telling that story on the phone forever. I love long stories. They remind me of the time I was thinking about a story that was longer than the usual stories I tell, but only by a little bit, since I didn't want people to get bored, though I think I forgot to tell the middle of the story, or maybe it was the end of the sto

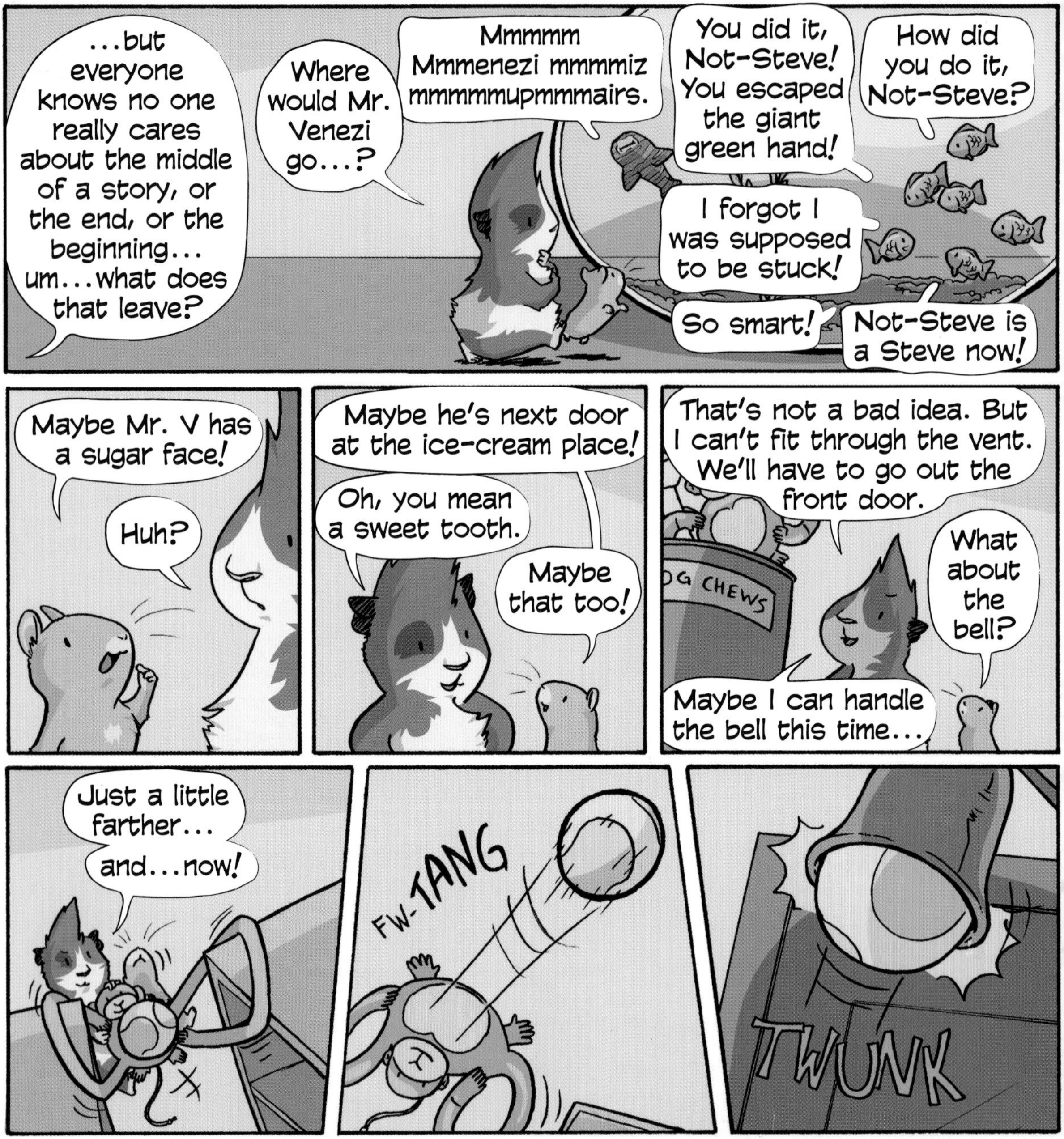
...but everyone knows no one really cares about the middle of a story, or the end, or the beginning... um...what does that leave?
Where would Mr. Venezi go...?
Mmmmm Mmmenezi mmmmiz mmmmmupmmmairs.
You did it, Not-Steve! You escaped the giant green hand!
How did you do it, Not-Steve?
I forgot I was supposed to be stuck!
So smart!
Not-Steve is a Steve now!
Maybe Mr. V has a sugar face!
Huh?
Maybe he's next door at the ice-cream place!
Oh, you mean a sweet tooth.
Maybe that too!
That's not a bad idea. But I can't fit through the vent. We'll have to go out the front door.
OG CHEWS
What about the bell?
Maybe I can handle the bell this time...
Just a little farther... and...now!
FW-TANG
TWUNK

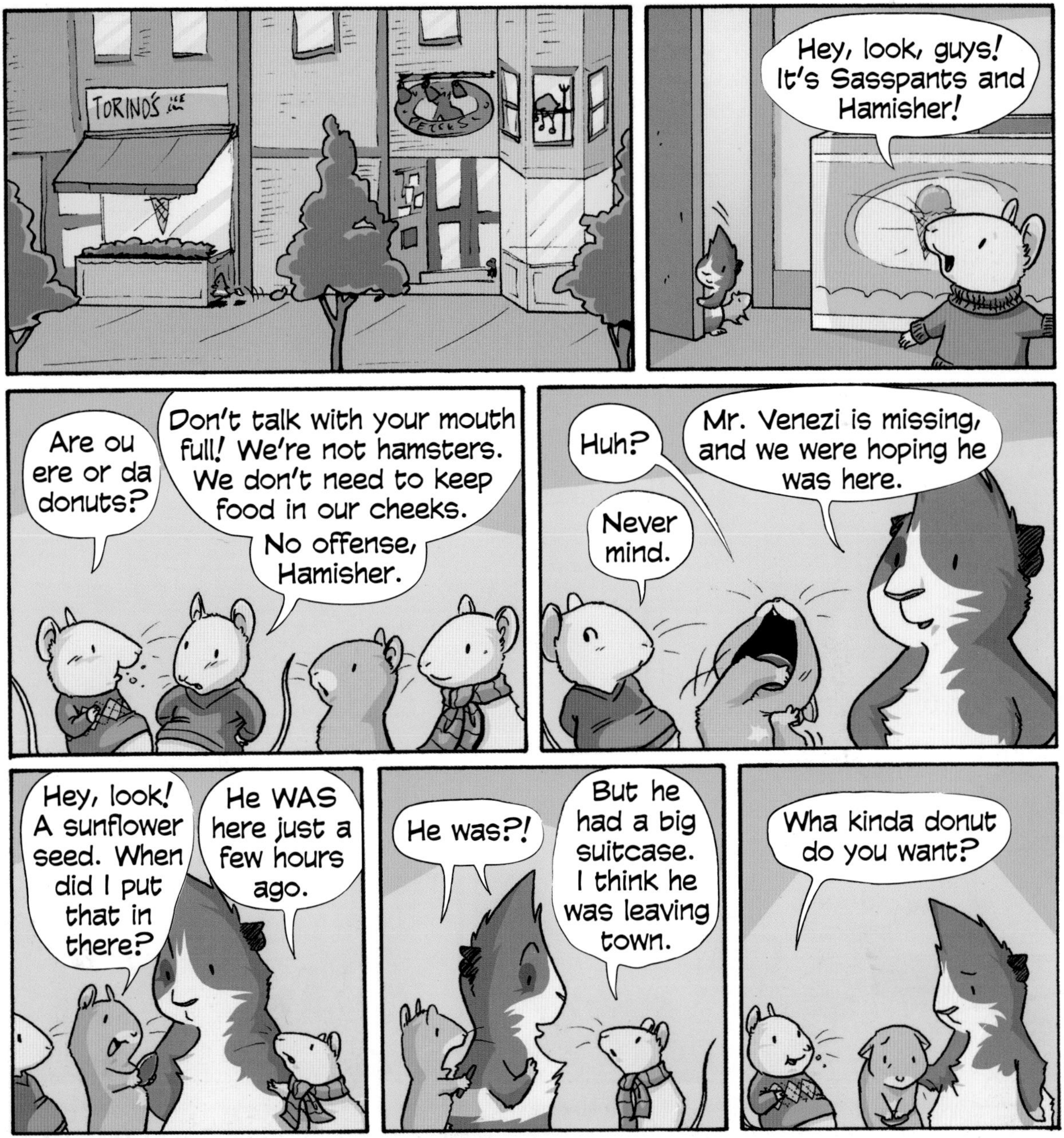
TORINO'S
PETER'S
Hey, look, guys! It's Sasspants and Hamisher!
Are ou ere or da donuts?
Don't talk with your mouth full! We're not hamsters. We don't need to keep food in our cheeks.
No offense, Hamisher.
Huh?
Never mind.
Mr. Venezi is missing, and we were hoping he was here.
Hey, look! A sunflower seed. When did I put that in there?
He WAS here just a few hours ago.
He was?!
But he had a big suitcase. I think he was leaving town.
Wha kinda donut do you want?

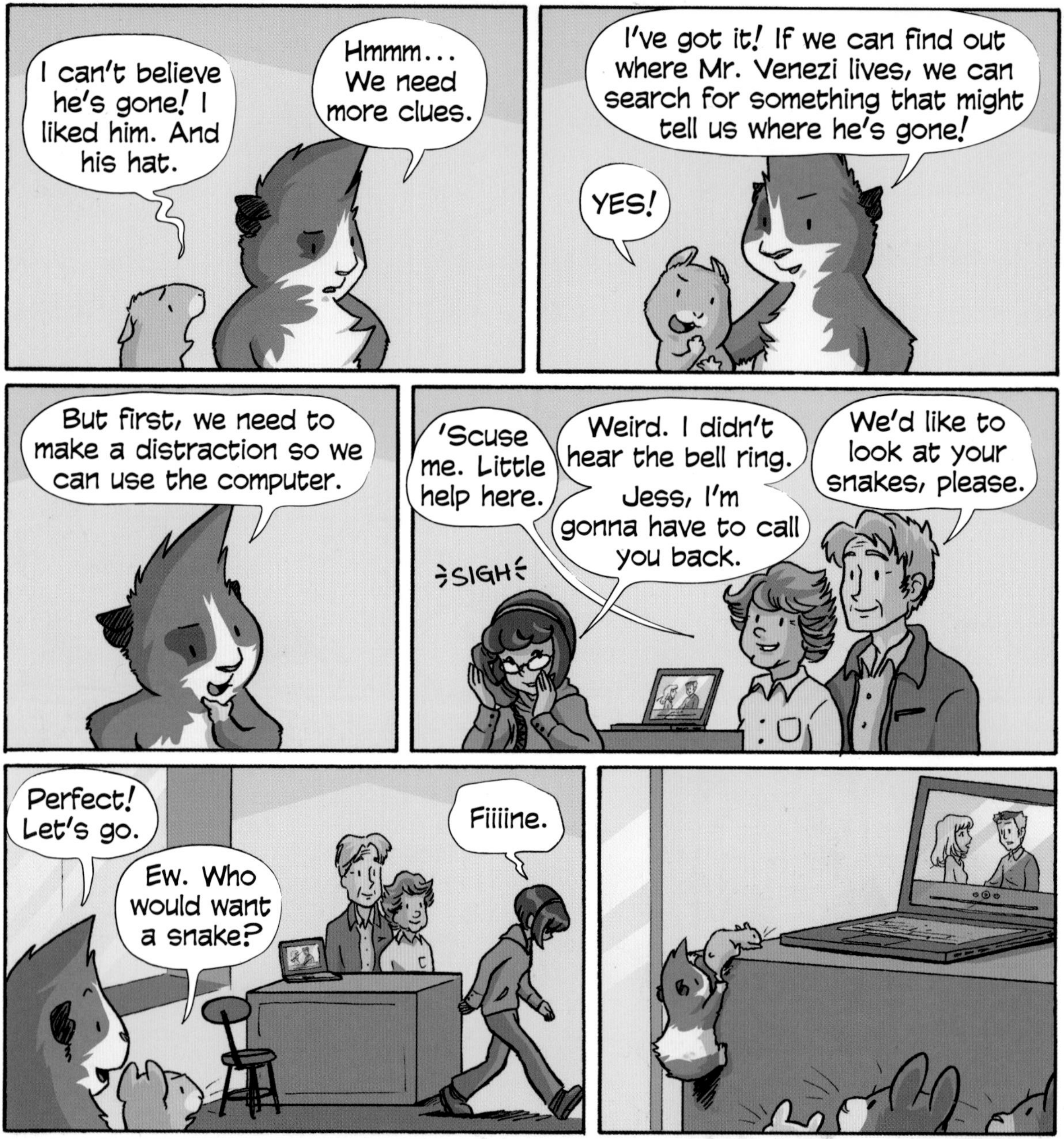
I can't believe he's gone! I liked him. And his hat.
Hmmm... We need more clues.
I've got it! If we can find out where Mr. Venezi lives, we can search for something that might tell us where he's gone!
YES!
But first, we need to make a distraction so we can use the computer.
'Scuse me. Little help here.
Weird. I didn't hear the bell ring.
Jess, I'm gonna have to call you back.
We'd like to look at your snakes, please.
SIGH
Perfect! Let's go.
Ew. Who would want a snake?
Fiiiine.

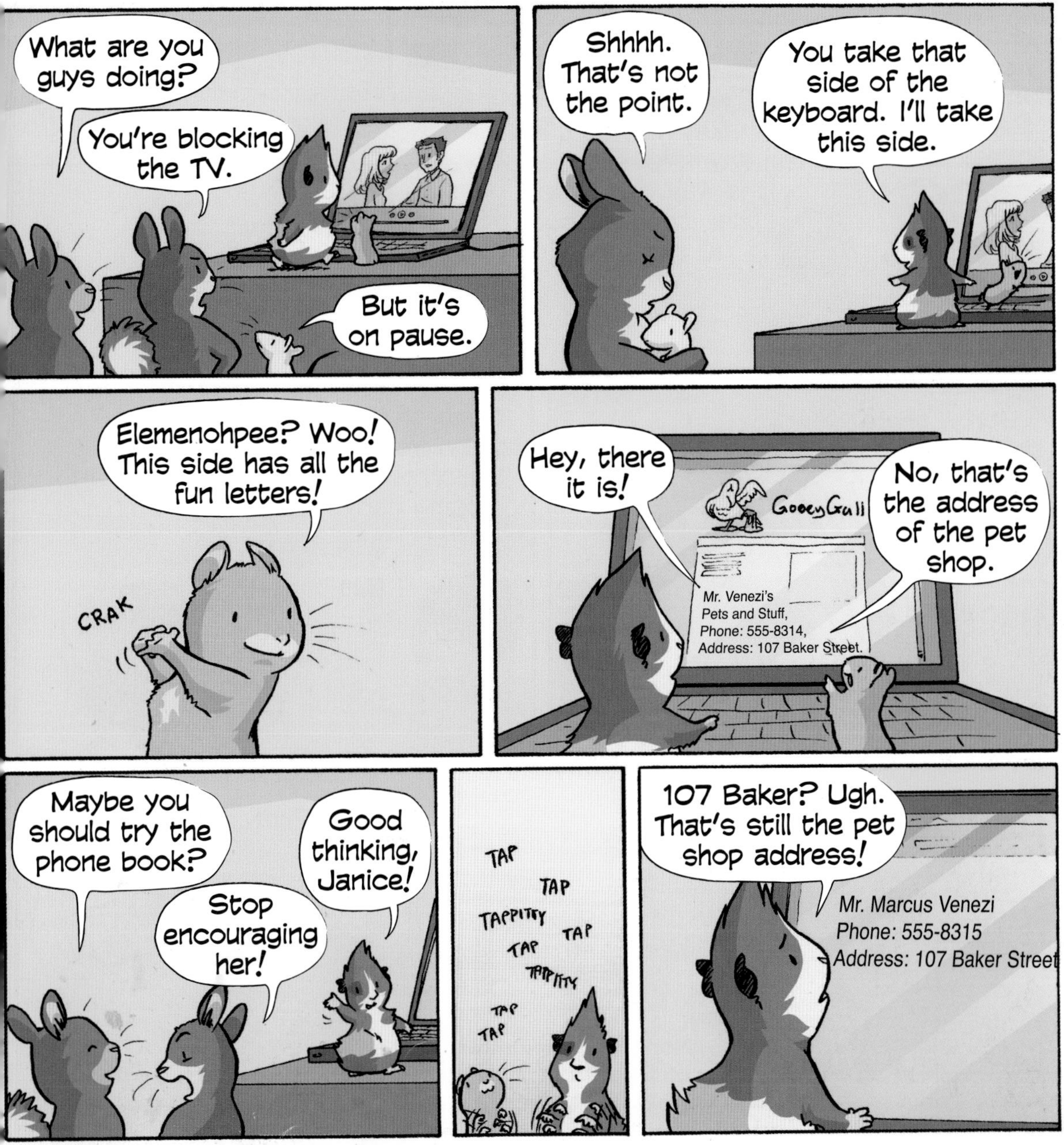
What are you guys doing?
You're blocking the TV.
But it's on pause.
Shhhh. That's not the point.
You take that side of the keyboard. I'll take this side.
Elemenohpee? Woo! This side has all the fun letters!
CRAK
Hey, there it is!
GooeyGull
Mr. Venezi's
Pets and Stuff,
Phone: 555-8314,
Address: 107 Baker Street.
No, that's the address of the pet shop.
Maybe you should try the phone book?
Stop encouraging her!
Good thinking, Janice!
TAP
TAP
TAPPITTY
TAP
TAP
TAPPITTY
TAP
TAP
107 Baker? Ugh. That's still the pet shop address!
Mr. Marcus Venezi
Phone: 555-8315
Address: 107 Baker Street

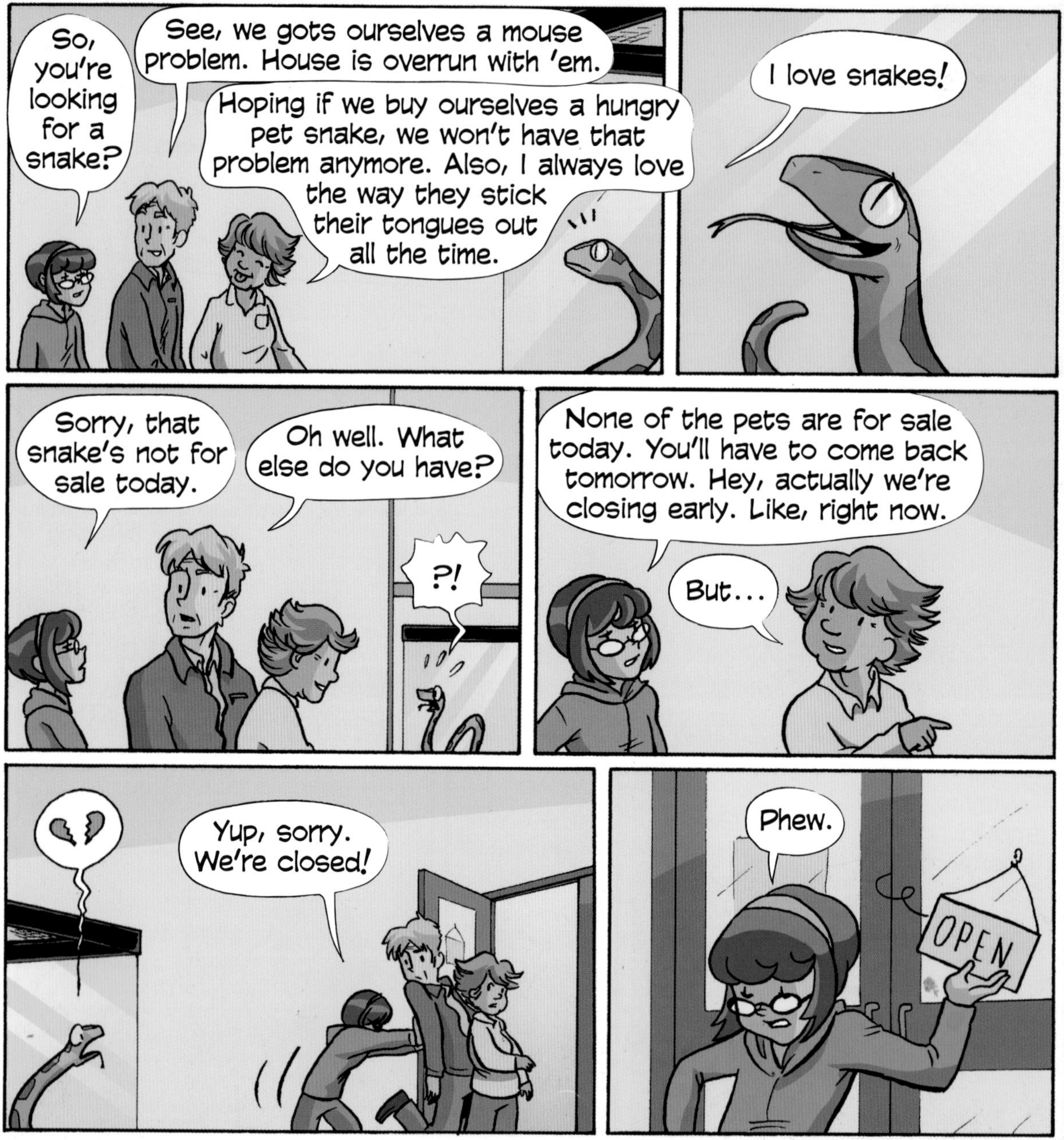
So, you're looking for a snake?
See, we gots ourselves a mouse problem. House is overrun with 'em.
Hoping if we buy ourselves a hungry pet snake, we won't have that problem anymore. Also, I always love the way they stick their tongues out all the time.
I love snakes!
Sorry, that snake's not for sale today.
Oh well. What else do you have?
?!
None of the pets are for sale today. You'll have to come back tomorrow. Hey, actually we're closing early. Like, right now.
But...
Yup, sorry. We're closed!
Phew.
OPEN

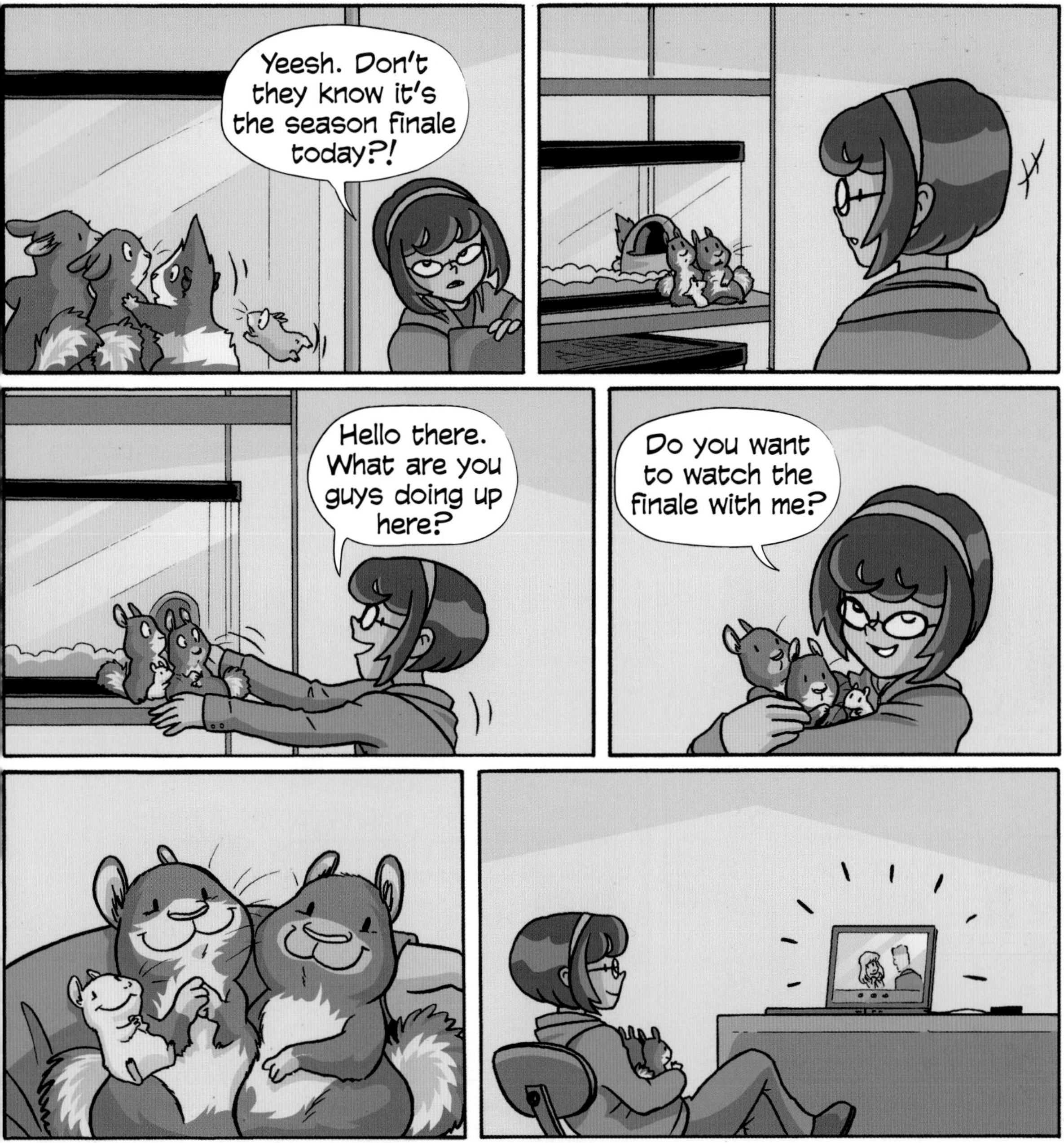
Yeesh. Don't they know it's the season finale today?!
Hello there. What are you guys doing up here?
Do you want to watch the finale with me?

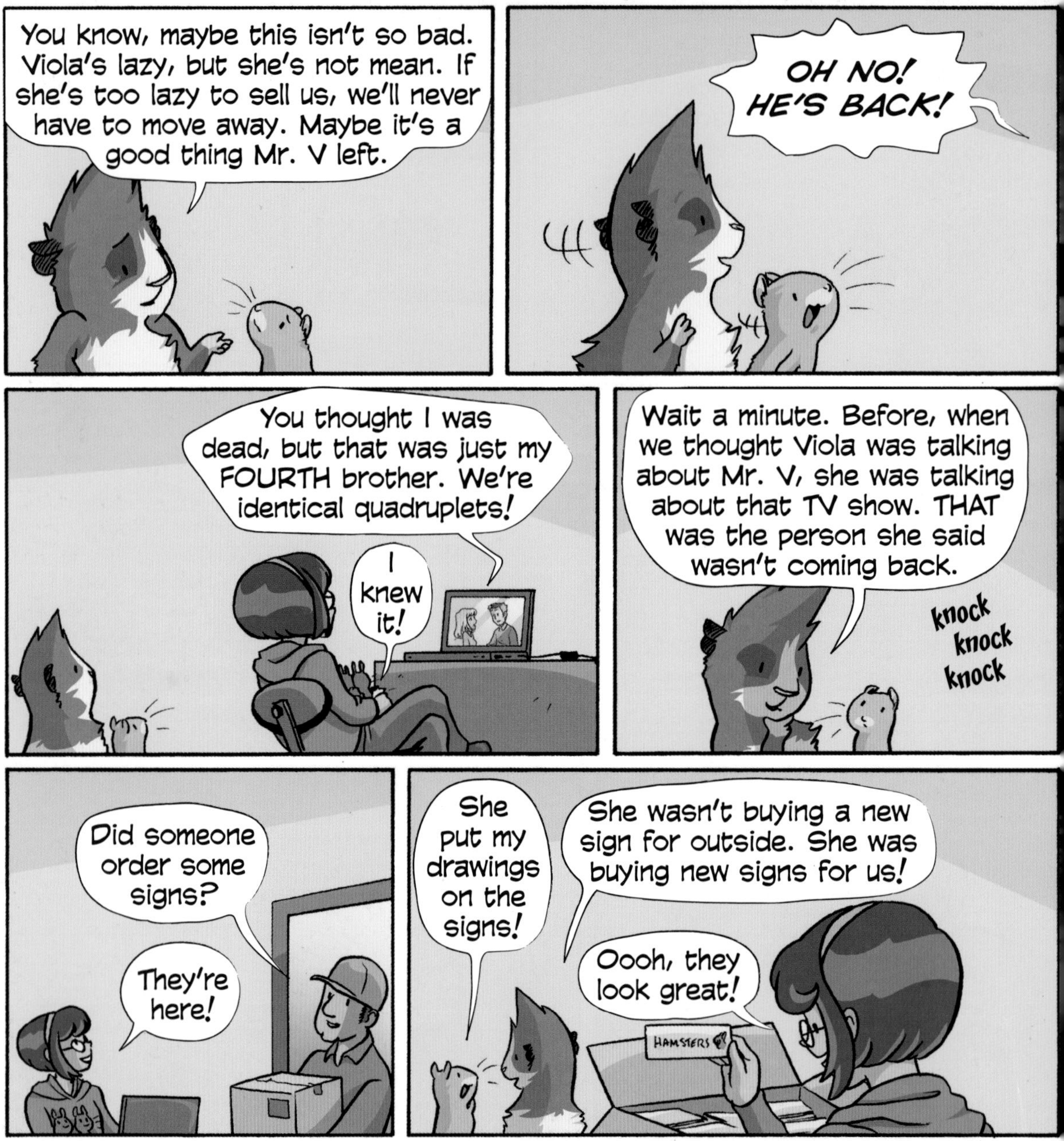
You know, maybe this isn't so bad. Viola's lazy, but she's not mean. If she's too lazy to sell us, we'll never have to move away. Maybe it's a good thing Mr. V left.
OH NO! HE'S BACK!
You thought I was dead, but that was just my FOURTH brother. We're identical quadruplets!
I knew it!
Wait a minute. Before, when we thought Viola was talking about Mr. V, she was talking about that TV show. THAT was the person she said wasn't coming back.
knock knock knock
Did someone order some signs?
They're here!
She put my drawings on the signs!
She wasn't buying a new sign for outside. She was buying new signs for us!
Oooh, they look great!
HAMSTERS

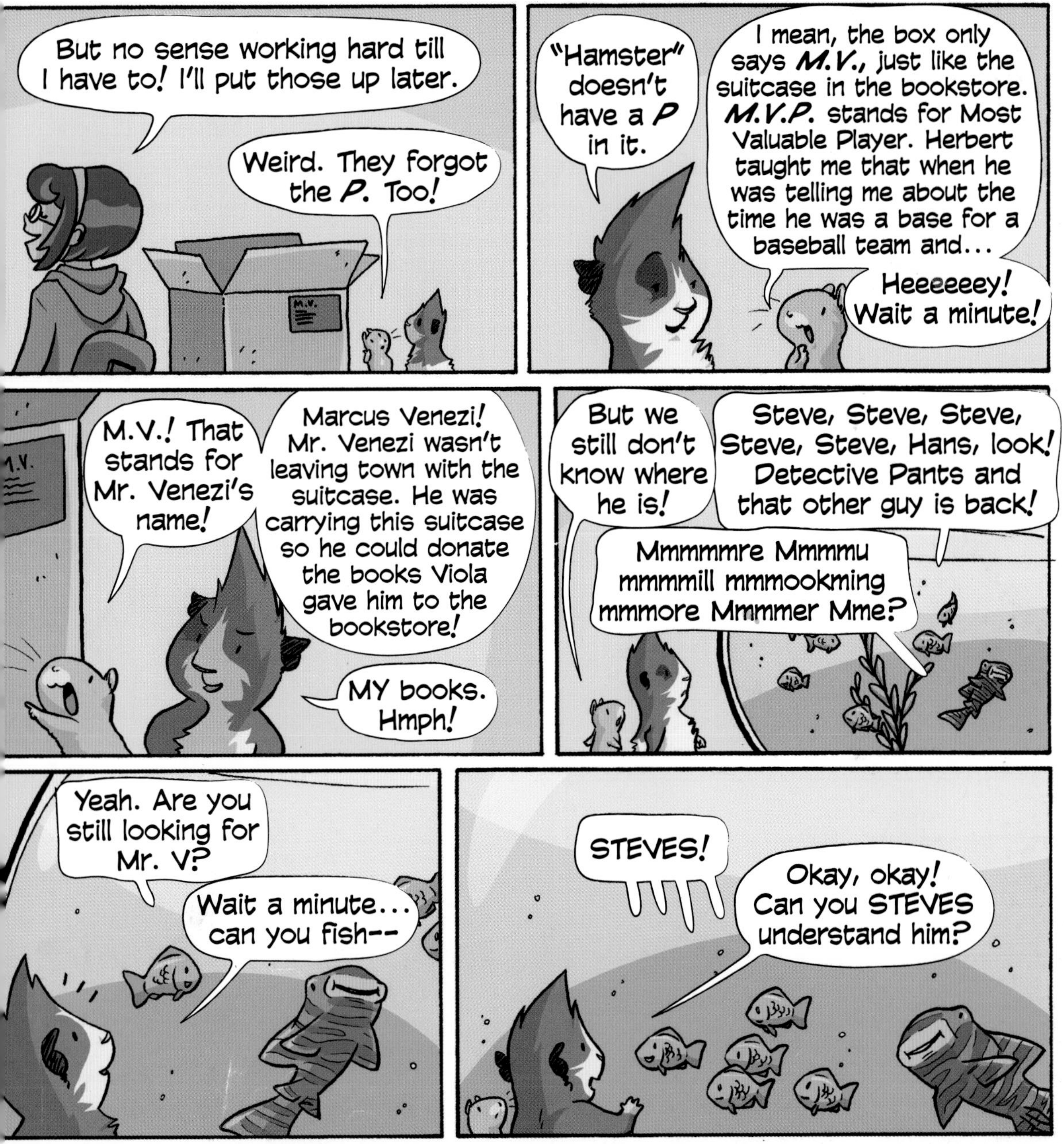
But no sense working hard till I have to! I'll put those up later.
Weird. They forgot the *P*. Too!
M.V.
"Hamster" doesn't have a *P* in it.
I mean, the box only says ***M.V.***, just like the suitcase in the bookstore. ***M.V.P.*** stands for Most Valuable Player. Herbert taught me that when he was telling me about the time he was a base for a baseball team and...
Heeeeeey! Wait a minute!
M.V.! That stands for Mr. Venezi's name!
Marcus Venezi! Mr. Venezi wasn't leaving town with the suitcase. He was carrying this suitcase so he could donate the books Viola gave him to the bookstore!
MY books. Hmph!
But we still don't know where he is!
Steve, Steve, Steve, Steve, Steve, Hans, look! Detective Pants and that other guy is back!
Mmmmmre Mmmmu mmmmill mmmookming mmmore Mmmmer Mme?
Yeah. Are you still looking for Mr. V?
Wait a minute... can you fish--
STEVES!
Okay, okay! Can you STEVES understand him?

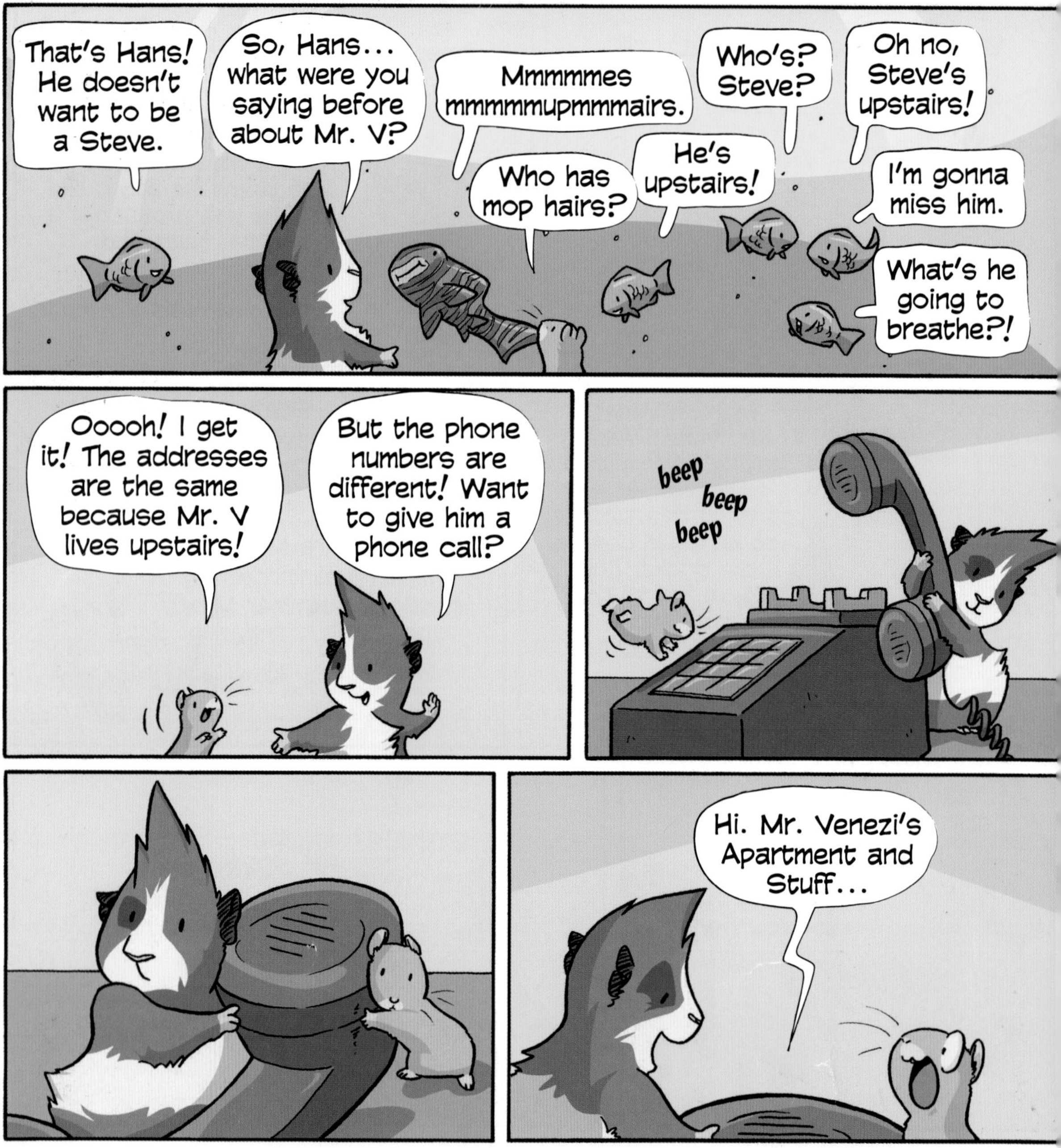
That's Hans! He doesn't want to be a Steve.
So, Hans... what were you saying before about Mr. V?
Mmmmmes mmmmmupmmmairs.
Who has mop hairs?
He's upstairs!
Who's? Steve?
Oh no, Steve's upstairs!
I'm gonna miss him.
What's he going to breathe?!
Ooooh! I get it! The addresses are the same because Mr. V lives upstairs!
But the phone numbers are different! Want to give him a phone call?
beep
beep
beep
Hi. Mr. Venezi's Apartment and Stuff...

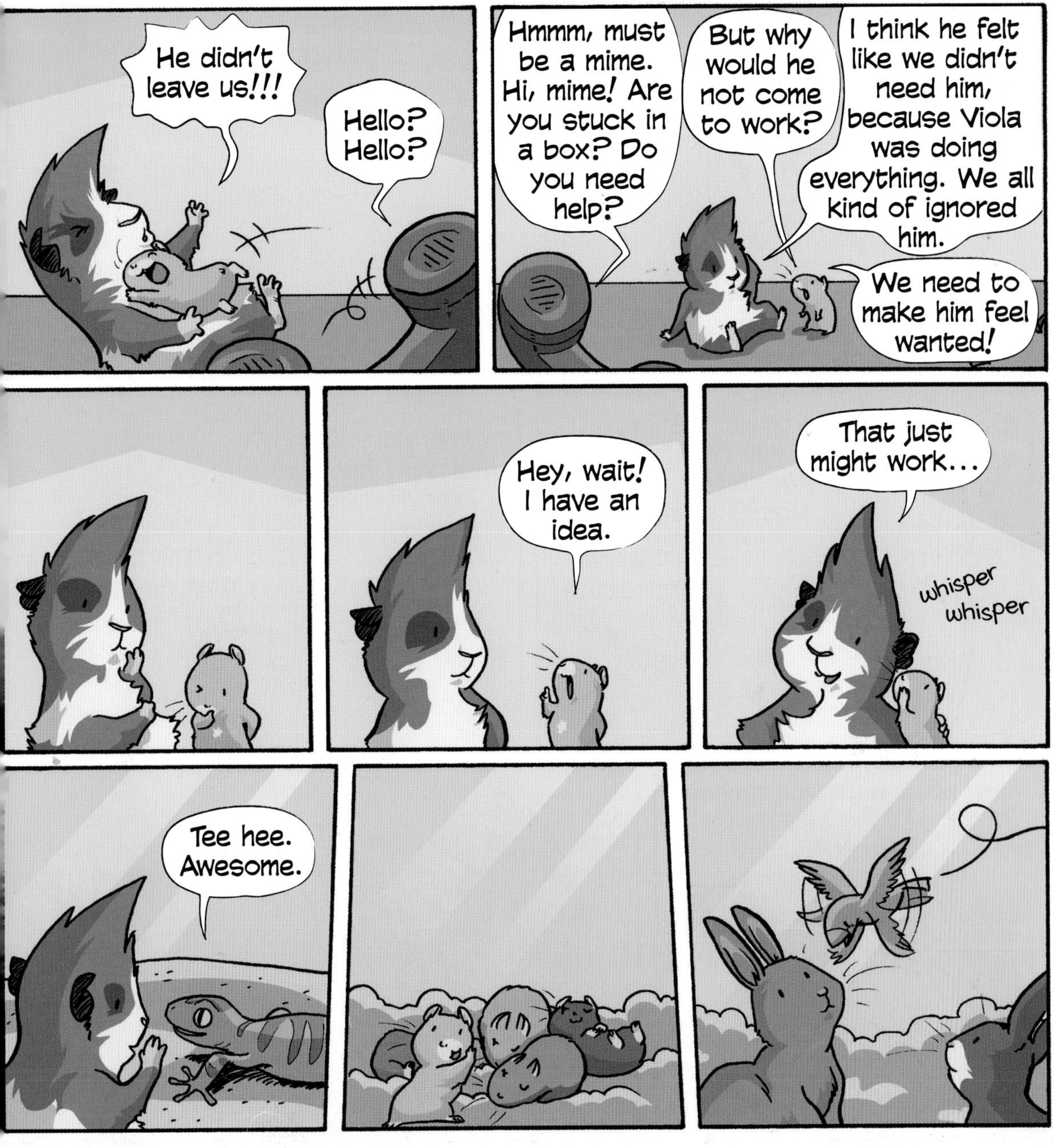
He didn't leave us!!!
Hello? Hello?
Hmmm, must be a mime. Hi, mime! Are you stuck in a box? Do you need help?
But why would he not come to work?
I think he felt like we didn't need him, because Viola was doing everything. We all kind of ignored him.
We need to make him feel wanted!
Hey, wait! I have an idea.
That just might work...
whisper whisper
Tee hee. Awesome.

We need a little help first.

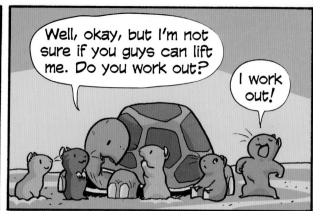

Well, okay, but I'm not sure if you guys can lift me. Do you work out?

I work out!

But I just escaped.

It's okay! We'll go with you this time! We can all be Not-Steves!

Thanks, Not-Steve!

Good thinking, Not-Steve!

What do you say, Gerry? I know you like Viola but--

Viola, Who? Name means nothing to me.

Now what were you saying about getting Mr. Venezi back?

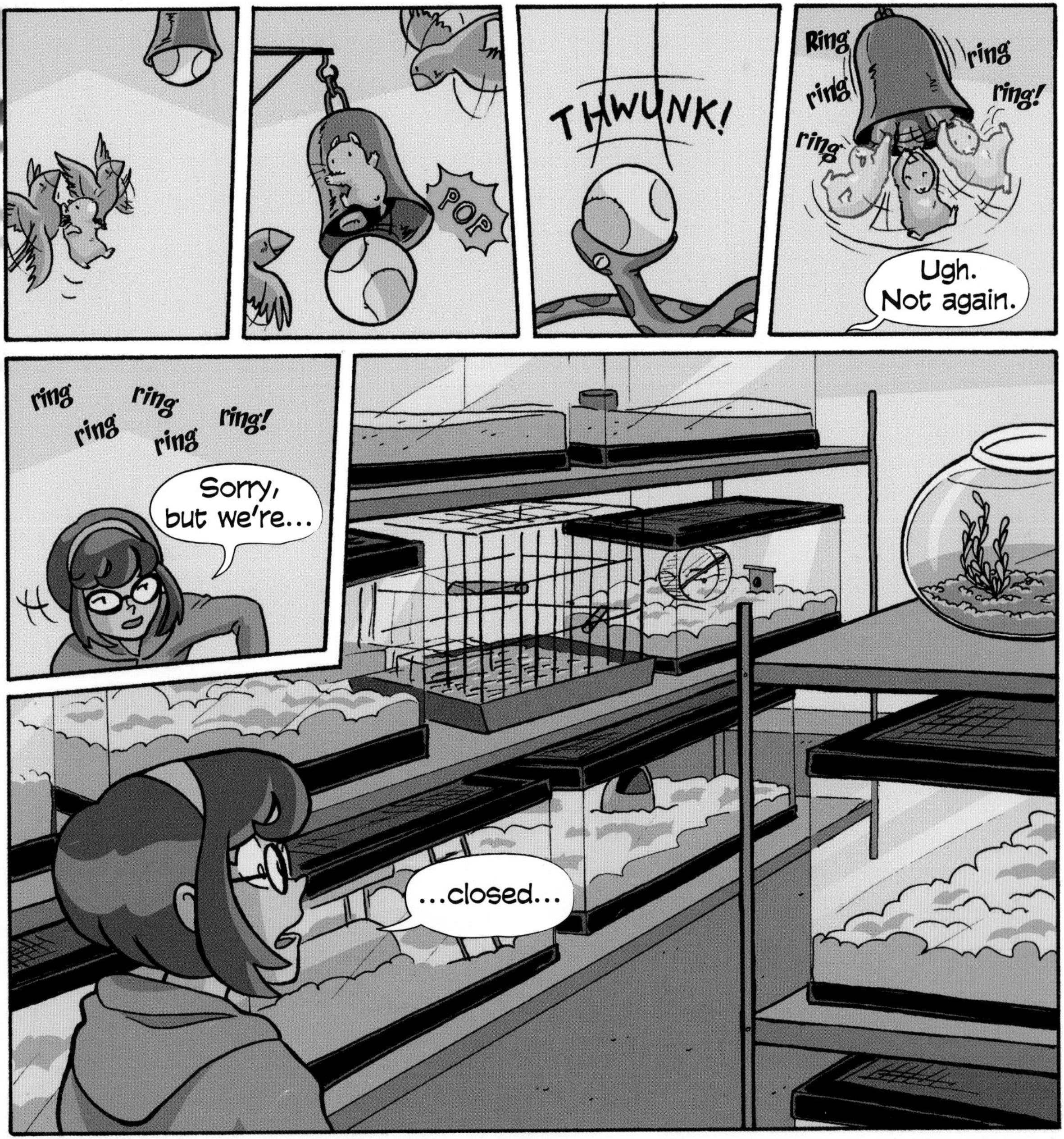
POP
THWUNK!
Ring
ring
ring
ring
ring!
Ugh. Not again.
ring
ring
ring
ring
ring!
Sorry, but we're...
...closed...

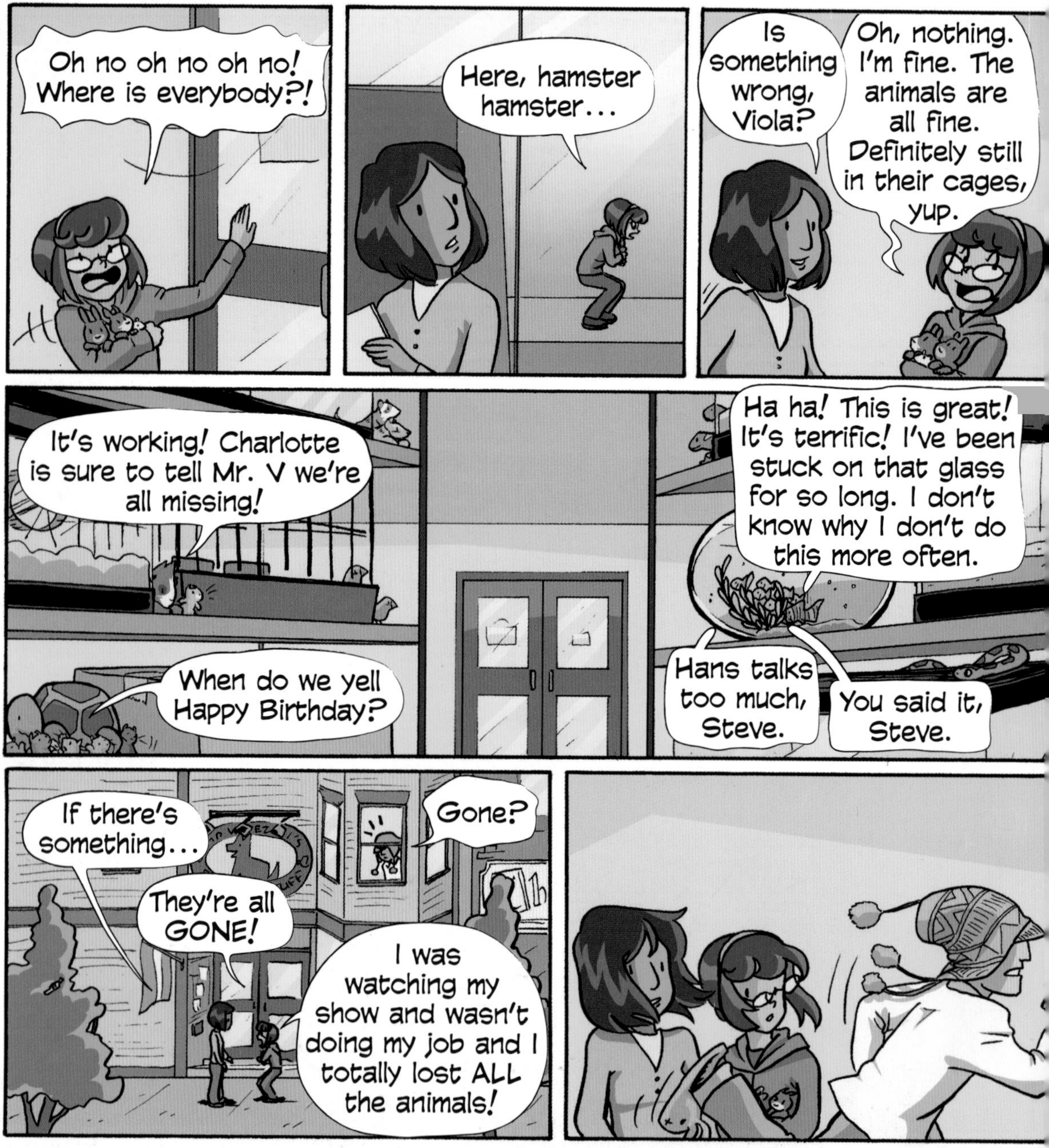
Oh no oh no oh no! Where is everybody?!
Here, hamster hamster...
Is something wrong, Viola?
Oh, nothing. I'm fine. The animals are all fine. Definitely still in their cages, yup.
It's working! Charlotte is sure to tell Mr. V we're all missing!
When do we yell Happy Birthday?
Ha ha! This is great! It's terrific! I've been stuck on that glass for so long. I don't know why I don't do this more often.
Hans talks too much, Steve.
You said it, Steve.
If there's something...
They're all GONE!
Gone?
I was watching my show and wasn't doing my job and I totally lost ALL the animals!

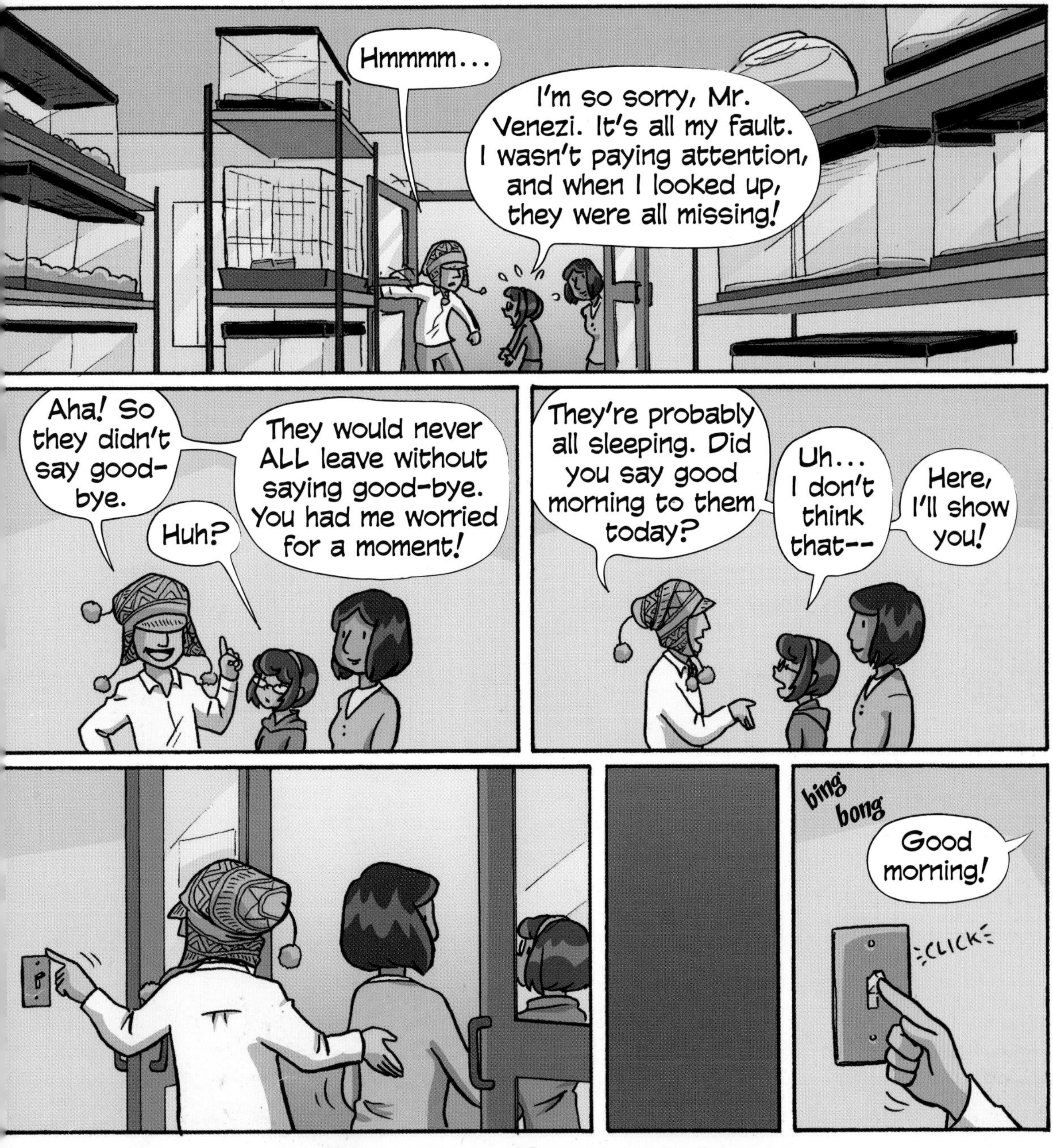
Hmmmm...
I'm so sorry, Mr. Venezi. It's all my fault. I wasn't paying attention, and when I looked up, they were all missing!
Aha! So they didn't say good-bye.
Huh?
They would never ALL leave without saying good-bye. You had me worried for a moment!
They're probably all sleeping. Did you say good morning to them today?
Uh... I don't think that--
Here, I'll show you!
bing
bong
Good morning!
CLICK

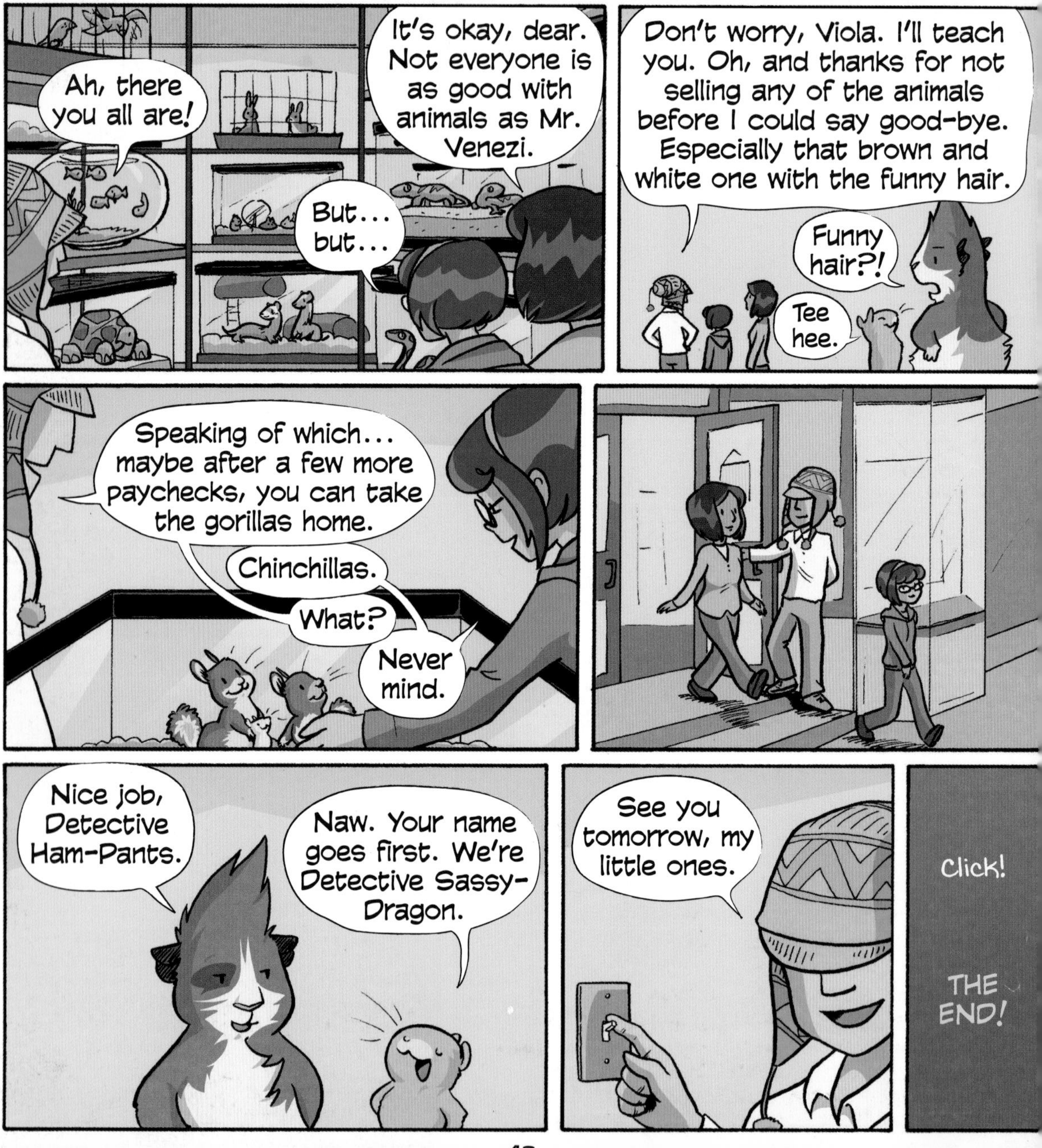
Ah, there you all are!
It's okay, dear. Not everyone is as good with animals as Mr. Venezi.
But... but...
Don't worry, Viola. I'll teach you. Oh, and thanks for not selling any of the animals before I could say good-bye. Especially that brown and white one with the funny hair.
Funny hair?!
Tee hee.
Speaking of which... maybe after a few more paychecks, you can take the gorillas home.
Chinchillas.
What?
Never mind.
Nice job, Detective Ham-Pants.
Naw. Your name goes first. We're Detective Sassy-Dragon.
See you tomorrow, my little ones.
Click!
THE END!

HAMISHER EXPLAINS...

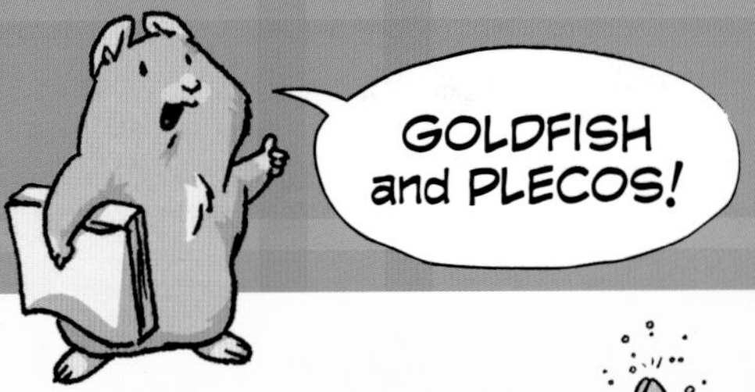
GOLDFISH
and PLECOS!

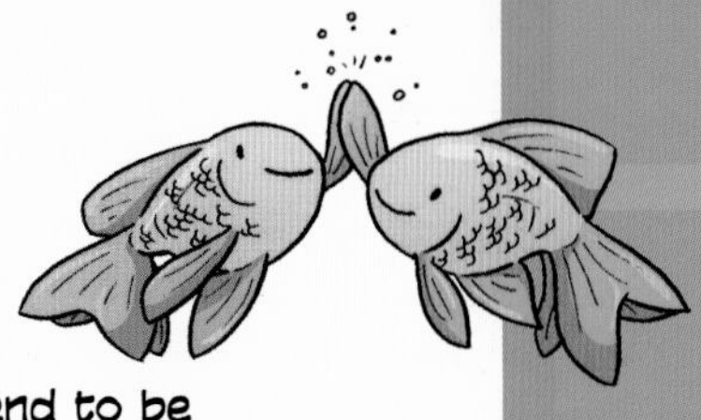

Fish may not be as cuddly or huggable as, say, a hamster or a dragon, but they make awesome pets!

The Steves are a type of goldfish called comets. It's hard to tell the difference between a girl and a boy goldfish, especially when they are all named Steve, but one way to tell is by looking at the pectoral fins. Girl goldfish tend to be bigger, and their pectoral fins are more rounded than on a boy goldfish.

Goldfish were around in Ancient China—and they were silver! Every now and then a fish would be born another color. When people put those goldfish together, the fish kids turned out to be more colorful too! Before long, there were lots of different colors of goldfish!

In the 1800s, goldfish were brought to Europe. People heated the fish tanks with open flames, and they kept accidentally burning down their houses. Whoops! Goldfish didn't come to the United States until 1878. I can't blame them, since it's a REALLY long swim from Europe.

Goldfish can live to be five to ten years old, but one of the oldest ever was a British goldfish named Tish, who lived to be 43 years old! Whoa.

I bet you learned in school that a group of fish is called a school, but a group of goldfish is called a troubling. If you see a bunch of goldfish hanging out in leather jackets, watch out.

Hans the fish is a plecostomus, a type of catfish. People just call them plecos or plecs or suckermouth armored catfish.

Plecos originally came from South America. Some can grow to be over three feet long! Count the number of lines on your pleco's top fin (or dorsal fin). If it's more than ten, that pleco can grow to be a MONSTER PLECO!

Plecos are great for fish tanks because they like to eat algae. Algae is that green gross stuff that grows on the glass. Pleco mouths work like tiny vacuums, and their mouths are super strong. A pleco can hold onto a rock in a raging river. Can you imagine being able to do that? That would make catching the bus a whole lot more interesting!

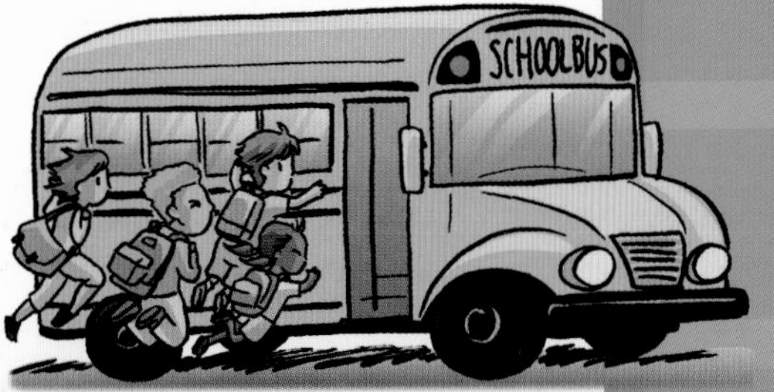
SCHOOL BUS

Jobs Working with Animals!

Viola works at the pet shop because she wants to be a veterinarian when she grows up. Even though she's a bit lazy, she does love animals. If you love animals too, there are tons of jobs you can have when you grow up! Here are a bunch of them:

SCIENTIST! People have to call you doctor, and you can twirl an imaginary mustache while you learn how to help animals. Marine biologists work with animals that live in water, such as dolphins, manatees, and sharks. Ornithologists work with birds. Herpetologists work with lizards and snakes. Ewww.

ANIMAL TRAINER! Some train dolphins to do backflips. Some train guide dogs and helper dogs. Some train famous furry movie stars. All of the trainers are great teachers!

PARK RANGER! Protect animals in their natural habitats and make sure that not too many pic-a-nic baskets get stolen.

DOG WALKER! Sometimes the dogs walk you!

GROOMER! Are you great at getting your hair just right? Can you pick out better outfits for Mr. Sparkles than Clarisse does?

WILDLIFE PHOTOGRAPHER! Or *FILMMAKER!* If you like taking pictures and making videos, why not practice on your pet? Maybe one of your Steves will go on to be a movie star.

ENVIRONMENTAL LAWYER! Do you like arguing with your sister when she's TOTALLY wrong? Environmental lawyers fight hard to make sure that places where animals live don't get messed up by people being mean or careless.

ZOOKEEPER! This is just like working at a pet shop . . . only these alligators are scarier than the "alligators" in Mr. V's shop! You can work with elephants, giraffes, lions, tigers, and bears. OH MY!